DIARY OF A BAKER'S SON

Cherry Danishes and Something About a Boy

Daniel Elijah Sanderfer

Blue Cottage Publishing

Copyright © January 2020 Daniel Elijah Sanderfer

Second Edition: July 2020

All rights reserved

The characters and events portrayed in this book are fictitious. Any similarity to real persons, living or dead, is coincidental and not intended by the author.

No part of this book may be reproduced, or stored in a retrieval system, or transmitted in any form or by any means, electronic, mechanical, photocopying, recording, or otherwise, without express written permission of the publisher.

Cover design by: Daniel Elijah Sanderfer
Cover photo by: Michael Rodichev
Edited by: Grayce Connors & Daniel Elijah Sanderfer
Printed in the United States of America

To every weirdo who has ever crushed on a boy.

DIARY OF A BAKER'S SON

by

DANIEL ELIJAH SANDERFER

CHAPTER ONE
Jeffrey

I love this time of year. The holidays are just around the corner and my mom is busy slaving away in her bakery. I work there on the weekends when I'm not in school and since we just let out for winter break, I've been spending more time there helping her.

Hi, I'm Jeffrey and I live with my mom Dana here in Clarksville, Indiana. When we moved here from Louisville a few years ago, my mom's shop was the only one in town. Now, the city is bursting at the seams with new business and plenty of competition. She worries a lot about paying the bills and making ends meet.

Business slowed over the summer and she had to cut back her staff, but she has high hopes that the holiday season will be the answer to her prayers. I've tried to help a little by creating a business page on Facebook and teaching her how to tweet but she's not very good at it yet, so I've sort of been managing our online presence by myself. I don't mind because it does bring in a few people every now and then, especially when she introduces a new donut or pastry. It's the last weekend before the Thanksgiving holiday so we've been working hard to create a buzz.

She had this brilliant idea to start selling homemade pies in an effort to help save people on cooking time and even though we've got a lot of likes on our social media, we won't know if the idea will pay off until a few days before Thanksgiving.

It was 6 A.M. Saturday; I yawned as we pulled up in front of the shop. She turned to me, "Ready for the day?" I rolled my head and stared at her with sleep still in my eyes. She tweaked my nose, "Thanks for being mommy's little helper." I felt my cheeks sear with blush as I slid down in the passenger's seat, crossed my arms, and pulled my beanie down over my face. She giggled, "I don't care how old you get, you will always be mommy's little helper."

I moaned, "Ma, I'm almost sixteen; I'm not a little boy anymore."

As she opened the car door she quipped, "To me, you will always be my little boy."

"Argh!" I grabbed my backpack and raced ahead of her to the front door of the bakery. She sauntered up behind me and unlocked the door. We stepped inside and I flicked on the lights then I dropped my backpack at a nearby booth.

She grabbed her apron from the kitchen just off the main counter, put it on, and started making the coffee from one of our two big restaurant-style coffee makers that sat on a counter directly behind the main display case. I've always loved the warm and inviting smell of brewing coffee but tend not to drink it much because it makes me super hyper. One Saturday morning after binge-watching Netflix until 4 A.M. I was practically crawling in the front door and ended up drinking six cups and mom called me the Energizer bunny for the rest of the day. Thankfully, we're only open from 6 A.M. till 1 P.M. and I crashed on the couch as soon as we got home. I honestly don't remember much else about that day except waking up from a nap at 5 P.M. that afternoon with a splitting headache.

Today, I was doing okay. I managed to get to bed at a fairly reasonable time, but I was still up later than normal reading the latest Julia McBryant novel and fantasizing about having a "daddy" of my own but then I realized, I don't care for spankings so I'd much rather find another boy.

My actual dad was a soldier in the U.S. Army and passed away when I was ten. He was on a special mission in Syria when his vehicle hit a roadside bomb. My mom still thinks about him every day and every once in a while, I'll hear her crying when she's in her room at night.

I was too young at the time to appreciate all the things fathers and sons do together and with him having been gone most of the time it's hard to remember a lot about him but I still miss him a lot. As I got older, and my body started maturing I could have used his help to answer a lot of questions I had like, "Why did I start growing hair down there?" and "What's that strange smell coming from my pits? Did I die or something?" I tried to talk to mom about these things but she'd get this nervous tick where she'd play with her hair and ask, "What's bringing all this up now?" so, I just said, "never mind" and kept all future boy problems to myself. I would love so much to have another boy I could talk to about these things, but I seriously doubt I'm going to run into one here at Dana's Delicious Danish.

Why "Danish" when we serve other things as well? Well, originally, mom only made Danish, but we weren't making enough money to pay the bills, so she added other menu items after that. Now, we also make pastries, cakes, cookies, pies, and cannoli. My favorite is still our cherry Danish, speaking of which, I think I'll go get one right now.

"Jeffrey!"

I slinked back to my seat with a snicker and my warm, delicious prize in hand. "Thanks, Mom!" An audible sigh echoed from the kitchen...

A lot of nice men come into the bakery and flirt with my mom. She always flatters them but when they leave, she tells me how dad was the only guy for her and she's not interested in being with anyone else. Oh, how I hope to find a guy like that one day.

You know what I mean. That special kind of guy that makes you hold your breath when he looks at you. A guy whose voice makes your insides turn to mush when he talks to you. *Sigh*... I want that so bad it hurts.

Mom knows I'm gay. I told her last year when I was going through a major bout of depression after my crush Van rejected me. I still play the moment over and over in my head like a TikTok video on loop. We were sitting on the bleachers after school doing our homework together, sharing whatever cookies or treats mom had made that morning.

Everyone at my new school seemed to be coupling up except me. Not to say I didn't try. I made the big mistake of telling this gorgeous, sweet, and funny, football player who came in the bakery every day that I had a crush on him. Prior to telling him how I felt, he would hang out with me after school all the time but afterward, he was really weirded out by it ... and I'm thinking about him again. *Argh*! Ok, so... when I said I was looking for a special guy? The one that makes me hold my breath when I think about him and my insides turn to mush? Well, that was Van. His buddies call him Van the Man.

So that day, he was sitting in the grass, legs crossed, his nose poked in his math book. I sat on the bleachers in front of him, legs together writing in my diary on my lap.

He broke the silence, "Hey Jeffrey, do you have any of those French cookies today?"

I glanced up with a smile and said, "Yeah." I set my diary aside and dug around in my backpack pulling out a baggie with some macaroons in it and tossed them his direction.

"Thanks, dude," he said as he yanked it open and began munching on them.

I don't why I was feeling so brave but then, we had been hanging out like this for weeks and I felt like there was something between us so I just said it; "I really like you, Van."

He looked confused for a minute then replied hesitantly, "I like you too, Jeffrey."

I sighed. Clearly, it was going to take me a few tries to get him to understand what I actually meant so I closed my diary, stood up, and sat down beside him in the grass while he mechanically continued making the macaroons disappear.

What happened next was an awkward mess destined for a barf inducing teen rom-com. I closed the math book in his lap and gazed right into his eyes, "No Van, I mean I *like you*, like you."

He swallowed hard and slid away, creating a gap between our legs as he mumbled, "Um, I'm not gay dude... but I'm totally flattered."

After an indeterminable amount of awkward silence, he quickly gathered his things, stood up, and said, "Catch you later dude." and headed off.

I sat there listening to the sound of my own heart popping like a balloon in my chest as I watched him walk away without so much as a glance back in my direction.

My mom tried to make me feel better when Van

stopped coming into the shop and talking to me, but it was little comfort knowing I was still going to see him every day at school.

    Inside, I secretly hope one day he will come around and confess his undying love for me, just like the guys eventually do in those stupid movies. But until that day happens, if it ever happens, I've stopped holding my breath, but it still hurts when I breathe every time I see him. He was the pause I needed in my life, the calm before the storm, my teenage dream.

CHAPTER TWO
Dear Diary

Dear Diary,
 Today I met a boy...
 I was working the front counter at the Triple D just past 9 a.m. on a Saturday like I normally do. The student crowd had come and gone for their morning caffeine and sugar fix so the only ones dwindling in now were the late risers and the few spontaneous customers suddenly deciding they would like something sweet.

The bell on the front door jingled and a well-dressed businessman stepped inside and glanced around. I was wiping off tables when I turned my gaze to a boy in black skinny jeans, a faded Zombies t-shirt and jet-black hair hanging mysteriously across his right eye who came in right behind him.

Upon further inspection, I noticed he had black marks drawn under his eyes and realized he was wearing makeup. I swallowed hard; he shook his head to style his hair without touching it. Fangirl scream, loudly, so loud it could shatter glass, but internally. I followed them to the counter and my voice cracked, "Good morning, can I help you?"

The man smiled, "I'll take a half dozen donuts, and whatever this guy wants?"

He stepped aside and the boy who had just made my heart poop its pants was standing right in front of me. His voice was deep and dark, like a cloudy day in autumn. "Do you have anything cream filled?"

I wanted to say "me" but seeing as how I had no idea who the man with him was I had to keep it PG. I'll spare you the details of what that possibly could have meant. I nodded and cleared my throat, "We have caramel and chocolate-covered Long Johns and donuts."

He poised his finger under his lip ring for a moment and flashed me a grin. I grabbed the napkin dispenser to balance myself because when he smiled I felt like I was going to pass out. How embarrassing would that be? Finally, he licked his lips and mumbled, "I'll have the chocolate-covered Long John."

"Great choice," I said with a crack in my voice.

What on earth is **wrong** with me? It's not like this is my first day speaking English! Did I lose what little sense I had? He watched me as I put on a fresh pair of gloves and shook open a new bag. I slid the Long John inside and handed it to him with a smile, which made him smile again.

"Stop it!" I shouted.

He snickered, "What?"

I could feel my cheeks sear with blush as I replied, "I'm so sorry, I meant **donut**!"

He pursed his lips, "Okay then."

His dad chuckled, "Quite alright buddy, how much will it be?"

"Nine dollars and eighteen cents."

He nodded, "That's a great deal."

As he handed me the cash he continued, "We just moved to town and we've been looking for a great place like this to satisfy our sweet tooth. Right son?"

The kid was busy sucking the cream out of his Long John, the sight of which made me have to shift myself to behind the non-see-through part of the counter. He replied with a sticky toned, "Yep."

As I handed the man his change, he smiled. "You two look to be about the same age. I bet you will be going to the same school."

I smiled big at the thought. "I go to Clark High."

The man tucked all but two dollars into his pocket, then handed the rest to his son, "Tip the boy JP."

He took the money and handed it to me. As he did, he lingered for a moment and my knees gave out, prompting me to drop slightly onto the counter. I shouted, "I'm okay!"

He arched a brow, "You sure?"

I nodded yes, but I was not okay. It was official, this was not a drill. I am so **not** okay. As they exited the bakery mom emerged from the kitchen, "How's everything going out here?"

I rushed to the window and watched them drive away and as I turned around, I pasted my back to the glass like a bug on a windshield and melted to the floor. Mom giggled, "Oh no, let me guess; it was a boy wasn't it?"

I whimpered like a puppy and mom shook her head, "Why do you torture yourself like this Jeffrey? If you thought he was cute, why didn't you ask him if he "wanted to hang" or whatever it is you kids do nowadays?"

I groaned, "It's not that easy mom. He was so cute, and dark, and mysterious, and…and…"

My words trailed off as I started to hyperventilate and mom tossed me a paper bag, "Jeffrey! Calm down, sweetie. It was just a boy!"

Once I regained my composure I replied, "He wasn't just **any** boy! He was totally adorable and I want to be the raincloud in his melancholy sky."

Mom smirked, "A Smashing Pumpkins reference?

Really Jeffrey?"

I lowered my head onto the table and mumbled, "He hit me like a bullet with butterfly wings."

Mom tousled my hair, "You cute little weirdo!"

"Argh! Is it time to go home yet?"

Mom flipped off the open sign and removed her apron, "Yeppers. We can go right after I close the register."

After a quick deposit at the bank, we made our way home. It was a nice house in a good neighborhood just a mile or two from the bakery. My parents bought it before I was born and we have lived there since. It's a cookie-cutter brick ranch that looks just like all the other houses around it, well, with the exception of mom's light decorating touch of bright pink shutters and a pastry theme wreath on the door. Even during the holidays, mom managed to incorporate baking in her décor. Our Thanksgiving's wreath features a giant turkey with a chef's hat. Festive!

On the way home, I took the chance to catch a brief nap. When we arrived, I excused myself to my bedroom to write a bit in my diary and then catch another nap while mom entered the daily profits into a spreadsheet and then took a long bath which was our usual Saturday after-work routine.

When I woke up, I expected mom to be in the tub but instead, she was still working on her laptop and looking a little worse for wear.

I yawned, "Are you okay mom?"

With a forced smile, she sighed, "I guess so."

I took a seat across from her on the loveseat. She sat her glasses and laptop on her desk then stood, crossed the room, and took a seat next to me. I was playing with my phone when she asked, "Whatcha looking at?"

"Funny videos," I mumbled.

She smiled, "I could use a little humor right now."

I set my phone down and turned to her, "You know you can talk to me about anything, I'm not a little kid anymore."

She adjusted my bangs, "I know, I just don't want to stress you out with adulting stuff."

I shrugged, "You won't stress me out. I once went to school in PJ bottoms and lived so I can handle anything."

Mom chuckled, "How did you manage that?"

I sank down a little, "I missed my alarms and forgot to change before leaving the house."

She shook her head, "Boy, your father and I gave you our best qualities, your father's devilish good looks, and my awkwardness. It was like God said, 'You're just too cute so, to keep you humble, I'm making you weird.'"

I smiled big, "Thanks mom, I'll be sure to put that on my dating profile when I get older."

She gestured in the air, "Ah, I can see it now. *One gorgeous guy in his prime with the looks of Brad Pitt and the awkwardness of Zoey Deschanel. If you're old enough to remember Hannah Montana, then I'm your guy!*"

A look of contemplation invaded my expression as I replied, "Perfect! Now let's figure out yours."

Mom waved in dismissal, "Oh please!"

I gestured grandly, "*Single baker looking for the perfect ingredients to create something special. Must like kids and know what a Champagne Supernova is!*"

"An Oasis reference? Really Jeffrey?"

I shrugged, "You played *Wonderwall* at your wedding. Just saying."

Mom covered her face. She was laughing so hard no sound was coming out. Once she regained her composure, she wrapped me in a hug, "You're going to make some boy very happy one day."

I closed my eyes to bask in her affection and mumbled, "Do you *really* think so?"

She separated from me, "I *know* so."

I reached for my phone and we went back to the video I was watching and shared a few laughs. After a few minutes, she sighed again, "I really hope this Thanksgiving pie pick up thing works out. If we don't make enough profit to catch up on the lease we'll have to close the shop."

I frowned, "Don't worry mom, everything is going to be okay and even if we have to close… at least we'll still have each other."

She flashed me a half-smile, "When did you get so wise?"

I shrugged, "I dunno."

She shook her head, "How about we order some pizza and binge watch some retro comedy shows?"

We were silent for a moment before my lips formed a smile, "Golden Girls?"

Mom grinned, "*Picture this: Sicily, 1924…*"

I laughed as she ordered the pizza and I set up the TV…

After dinner, and who knows how many St. Olaf stories, we fell asleep in our respective places in the living room. At some point she woke me up and I slinked down the hallway to my room.

Dear Diary,

Today mom told me that if we didn't make enough money from the Thanksgiving pie promotion we would have to close the Triple D.. I'm trying not to freak out but it's hard. I wish I could do more to help, but what am I supposed to do when I have school?

I could just drop out and work full time… I should prob-

ably finish my education though since I've made it this far. I mean I only have like three years to go before I graduate. Argh! I don't know what to do.

Maybe I can think better in the morning. I could always punch up our social media presence. That's it! That's what I can do! More Instagram, and Facebook posts; I think I have some pictures on my phone.

Ttyl -Jeffrey

  I flipped open my phone. I had lots of pictures of mom's test pies but she told me not to share them because they weren't exactly perfect. I bit my bottom lip and thought for a minute. I picked the best-looking pumpkin pie, put a cute fall border around it, then posted it to Insta with the hashtags #danasdeliciousdanishes #danasholidaypies #tripledpies #tripledholidaypies *"Frozen pies are lies! Why not pick up something fresh to serve your family this holiday season? You can even tell everyone you baked them yourself! Your secret is safe with us!"* Within a few minutes, my notifications started going crazy. Un-freaking-believable! I couldn't wait to tell mom in the morning that her pies were going viral with likes and comments!

  Still in my PJs from earlier, I climbed into bed. As I laid down and burrowed under my blankets like a mole my IG messenger chimed; *"John Phillip Richards would like to send you a message."*

  Normally, I would wait until the morning but for some reason, I couldn't resist checking it. Most of the time it was some older guy on IG making a pass at me, but lo and behold, as I opened my IG back up and went to my messages, I saw the picture and sprung up in my bed.

  Oh my god! It was *him*! It was the boy from the bakery! With trembling fingers, I read the words he typed...

  "Hey, it's JP I was at your bakery today with my dad. That long *john was the best one I've ever eaten, can't wait to pick up another one tomorrow!"*

Heavy breathing! Glass shatters! Literally *dead*! He was coming back tomorrow, and I would be there working! As I "inner fangirl screamed" another message came through...

"I was going to say I didn't catch your name earlier but since you posted from the name Jeffrey Towler am I safe to assume you're not using an alias?"

I quickly replied, *"Nope. Jeffrey is my real name."* To cover up the pause that followed I added, *"Don't wear it out."*

Earth-shattering inner scream! *Where is the delete button? Unsend! Unsend! Argh! Somebody KILL me!* I tossed the phone on my nightstand, fell back onto my bed, and covered my face with my pillow. Just as I was utterly convinced that I had totally blown it with my utter lameness, another *ding*! I hurriedly rolled over to grab it but knocked it halfway across the room onto the floor with a loud *thump*! A few minutes later mom shouted from her room next to mine, "Jeffrey, are you okay in there?"

My head popped up from the other side of the bed, hair sticking up in all directions, "I'm okay!"

"Okay then, keep it down, Goodnight!"

"Goodnight mom!" I climbed back into my bed and opened my messages again...

"LOL"

LOL? That was *IT*? Wait... he thought it was funny. That's good, right? Hello? Reader? HALP!

Arching my brow, "Your silence is deafening. Fine then. I see how it's going to be. One of those guardian angel type things where you're not allowed to intervene, just watch the events play out. Argh!"

Fine then, I'll just ask the author! "Daniel, I really want a chance with this boy. Can I please have a chance with this boy?"

"*We'll see.*"

"So, is that a maybe?"

"*I'm really not supposed to be talking to you during the story where others can see it.*"

"Um, hello! You created me so if I can't ask you for help then who else can I turn to?"

"*Shouldn't you be sending JP another message?*"

Eep! I grabbed my phone and replied, "*That was pretty cheesy right?*"

A few seconds passed... "*I like things that are cheesy, especially awkward boys who don't know what to say. See you tomorrow.*"

Flatline! Hashtag *dead*! Cut to me with a rose in my hand lying in my bed. But wait, I *can't* die in my pajamas! That would be such a crime, especially since the pajamas in question are nothing more than a pair of old track pants and a faded flannel shirt that belonged to my dad. Plus, if I died tonight, I wouldn't get the chance to see JP tomorrow. So, Goodnight Reader. Goodnight Daniel. Could someone get me a glass of milk from the kitchen? Oh yeah, fine, I'll go get it myself.

CHAPTER THREE
Breakfast at ~~Tiffany's~~ Dana's

Sunday morning. Yawn. Today is going to be a busy day at the bakery. With any luck, my social media campaign will hopefully bring in the masses. My only worry is how will mom and I handle the rush?

Pop! My head poked out from the sea of blankets and pillows at the sound of mom knocking on the door.

"Jeffrey, are you awake? We need to get to the bakery a little early this morning so we can prepare for the church folks and start prepping pies to bake."

"I'm awake, I'll be out shortly!"

Normally, I don't go in until around 6:00 a.m. to help mom with front-end set-up. But with us being short on help, I've started getting up at 2:30 so we can make it to the bakery and get everything ready before we open. I rolled out of bed and lazily scratched my butt cheek as I made my way to the door. Hello! Um, reader could you turn away for a minute. I have a bad case of morning wood and would really prefer no one to see it. Go grab a snack or something okay?

Sorry about that. Being a sixteen-year-old boy is *so* much fun sometimes let me tell you. Between the painfully awkward moments, the utter clumsiness, and the circus in my pants I feel like a sideshow freak most of the

time. In the shower, I made mindless circles with the soap around my chest as I smiled and thought about JP *Plop! Whoops!* I dropped the soap. *Squeak! Thump!*
"Jeffrey, are you alright in there?"
"I'm alright!"
Cut to me, hair sticking up in all directions peeking over the edge of the tub. Yeah, yeah, if you must know what happened, I slipped on the bar of soap and tried to grab the water to keep from falling. Now, I'm standing in the mirror observing a big bruise developing on my butt. As if I didn't have enough awkwardness to deal with, I'm gonna be sitting funny for a few days until the initial pain subsides.

    I wrapped a towel around my waist and proceeded back to my room. Mom was in the kitchen fixing a quick breakfast. As I closed the door, I could feel the towel slip from my body. Peas and gravy! What else could go wrong today? (Yes, I know I have a mole on my left butt cheek thank you very much.)

    Argh! I removed the jammed towel from the door, closed it, and scrambled to my chest of drawers to grab a pair of tighty-whities, a pair of jeans, and a comfortable t-shirt. Slipping on my beat-up converse sneakers, I grabbed my Kindle, phone, hoodie, and backpack and made my way to the kitchen.

    Mom had fixed scrambled eggs and bacon for breakfast, but I opted to grab a Cherry Danish leftover from the bakery instead. I swiped one from the covered glass serving dish on the table and took a huge bite. Mom chuckled with delight as I munched away. She shook her head and approached with a washcloth to wipe the sticky redness from my face and lips. "Couldn't you have at least gotten a plate so you didn't risk ruining the carpet?" *Yes, we have carpet in my kitchen. Don't judge me.*

"No can-do ma! It was an emergency!"

"Cherry Danishes are not an emergency." She fired back.

I paused momentarily from my munching, "Blasphemy!"

She giggled, "You're a hot mess."

I grinned, "Yeah, but, I'm *your* hot mess!"

She shook her head with a smile as she carried her plate and coffee cup to the sink, "Yes, you are!"

After I made sure I had all of my gear tucked away in my backpack. At the same time, I was trying to lick some lingering cream cheese from the corner of my mouth. Finally, I just opted to wipe it off once I got my hoodie on. With a quick check of my phone, I shouted, "Holy crap on a cracker!"

"Jeffrey!" Mom shouted as she grabbed her keys off the entryway table by the front door.

"Sorry Ma, it's just I did a thing last night and well we may need some help today."

She arched her brow, "What do you mean?"

I lowered my gaze, "I kind of posted a picture of one of your pies to Insta, and we have over a hundred likes and comments."

She crossed the room and gazed at my phone screen, "Jeffrey, I thought I told you not to post those! they were just tests!"

"Well, it seems that people didn't mind because they all are planning to buy one. A lot of them are buying more than one!"

Mom and I met one another's gaze and our lips formed smiles. She shouted, "Jeffrey! What on *earth* are we going to do? We haven't even made a single one yet!"

I thought for a moment, "We'll figure it out, but we

better get to the shop and get started."

She shook her head and placed her hand behind my neck, "Did I ever tell you that you're my favorite kid?"

I frowned, "I'm an only child!"

"See? Works out perfectly," she said racing to the door. "Come on! We have a lot of baking to do!"

**

As I flicked on the lights and turned on the ovens, coffee makers, and other equipment, mom stood listening to the practically endless inquiries and order requests on the voicemail, her eyes getting wider with each message.

"Jeffrey are you *hearing* this?!"

I grinned.

"These are all pre-orders! We're looking at potentially hundreds of pies between all these messages!"

That's not counting all the requests on our social media!

"Oh my God, are we going to have time to make this many pies? She looked at the calendar on the wall behind her and did some math in her head. "Okay, we have three days to get it together. I can make around twenty pies in an hour, times eight hours... We might have to work a couple of nights, but we can pull this off!"

I chimed in, "I'll start returning calls and social media messages. I'll find out what they want when they're going to pick it up and charge their credit card. "

She cupped my face in her hands, "Brilliant!" She kissed my forehead, "Now what pies are we going to offer?"

I shouted, "Cherry, Pumpkin, Apple, and Pecan!"

Mom quickly went to check the pantry. She emerged, "We're good on crust ingredients but we're going to eventually need more fillings."

I shrugged, "We can stop by GFS today after we

close."

    She put on her apron, "Sounds like a plan to me."

    Before she went to work, she paused and met my gaze, "Thanks for all of your help baby."

    I shrugged, "What can I say, I'm just fabulous."

    We laughed and I went to set up my order station with a notebook and calculator (Math is not my strong suit.) right next to the phone and credit card machine. I hopped on the computer and whipped up a couple of cute signs to place on the front door and displays so our customers knew which pies we would be offering.

    As I tried to make more room for my station by finding a different place for our plastic dining trays, a familiar voice mumbled "Hey!" behind me and the trays exploded out of my hands and tumbled to the ground. In the rush of all the excitement, I had temporarily forgotten that JP said he would be coming by today!

    Cue earth-shattering scream. Mom rushed from the kitchen, "Jeffrey, are you okay?"

    With my hands still placed over my mouth, I turned to her and nodded. She smiled at JP behind me. "Oh, hi there! We're not open yet, but we have some leftover doughnuts and things from yesterday for 50% off if you're interested," she said as she made her way to get the coffee started.

    JP came over and bent down to help me pick up the trays scattered everywhere. "Actually, I don't mind waiting for fresh ones." Our eyes locked as he handed me his stack of trays. "I was kind of here to see Jeffrey."

    Mom's eyes blinked rapidly, "Oh."

JP flashed me a grin as he noticed my sharp intake of breath when our hands touched briefly during the tray exchange. In an attempt to cover I asked, "So, where's your dad?"

"Oh, he's just across the street. We bought the old florist's house."

I smiled in acknowledgment, but inside my mind, I totally fainted. He lives *across the street from our bakery*, meaning I will get to see him every day. Heavy breathing. Lump in throat. Why am I sweating so much? I'm losing so much moisture out of my palms. Need water!

Mom simply couldn't watch me struggle any longer. She turned to us and propped her elbows on the display counter. "So, JP is it? What are you doing up so early in the morning?"

He replied respectfully, "I'm always up this early. I like the night."

Mom pursed her lips, "Okay then. Does your dad know where you are?"

He nodded, "Yeah, he gets up to read the paper, check the stocks, and work out."

"I see." Mom replied. After a momentary pause, she asked, "What does he do for a living?"

"He's an investor," JP replied.

Mom turned to me, "Did you hear that Jeffrey? His dad is an investor. Fancy."

Turning her focus back to JP she asked, "Where's your mom?"

JP turned away and rubbed his elbow, "She's no longer with us. She was a pastry chef in Louisville before she passed. I used to help her bake sometimes."

Mom's expression dampened, "I'm so sorry."

"That's awesome," Mom said with a sympathetic smile.

He glanced down, "I used to help her bake a lot... if you ever need an extra set of hands."

He lifted his eyes and stared into mine hopefully. I

turned to mom and she thought for a moment before sighing, "We do have a lot of work for the holidays. I can't pay much but if it's okay with your dad we could really use some help preparing pies?"

His lips formed a smile as he pulled his phone from his pocket. "Can I call him?"

Mom smiled, "Well aren't you the little go-getter."

He shrugged, "Better than sitting home all day."

He stepped aside as mom whispered, "You know I normally wouldn't go for something like this but we really could use the help. Can you show him the ropes?"

If there was ever a time I was prepared to answer "yes" it was this one so I said it before she could barely finish the sentence.

JP approached and lifted his hands, "I'm all yours! Just give me an apron and some gloves."

Plop! A few minutes later I awoke staring at the ceiling. Mom was smacking my face, "Jeffrey! Jeffrey! Are you okay?"

I mumbled, "What happened?"

She tried to cover an oncoming smile, "You fainted."

I raised up and saw JP leaning coyly against the counter. He smirked, "All I said was I'm all yours."

Blackness again! When I came to mom quipped, "Jeffrey, are you okay?"

JP handed me a glass of water, "You might should talk to a doctor about that."

I took a sip, then handed the cup back to him. Mom grabbed my hand, "Alright now tippy tumbles, up and at em!"

JP grabbed my other hand and I made it to my feet. I stood for a moment and just breathed. Mom gave a thumbs up to JP "You got this buddy?"

JP gave her a thumbs up and a smile. I had totally forgotten I was still holding his hand. I glanced down, then up into his eyes and he smiled. "You can let go now if you're okay?"

But… I didn't *want* to let go. I had dreamed of this moment ever since I understood what a crush was and despite the fact we had only just met, something about standing there holding his hand and gazing into his big sad eyes felt so right. Slowly, I released him, but inside my heart was screaming "Nooooo!"

We stood in silence for a moment, our eyes danced awkwardly across the room. He was rubbing his arm as he said, "So, where should we start."

I attempted to clear the lump in my throat before replying, "Well, as mom gets things ready she'll ring the bell and slide a tray through the window behind us. We then take the tray and slide into the display."

He nodded, "That doesn't sound too hard. What happens when we run out of something?"

I grinned, "Then we're out."

He giggled, "Fair enough."

Just as I finished showing JP the basics on working the cash register, Mom poked her head through the window, "You boys ready?"

"Yep," I replied as she poked a tray through.

JP grabbed the tray, then passed it to me and I slid it into the display. A few trays of various doughnuts and Danish later the display was full. Mom emerged wiping her hands on her apron and checked the clock, "Looks like it's that time."

JP asked, "What time?"

She tousled his hair, "Time to open silly."

He grinned, "Oh."

I made my way to the window, turned on the open sign then made my way back behind the counter. Mom was across the room getting a cup of coffee. She added cream and sugar then stirred it before taking a sip. As she made her way back to where we were standing she said, "So, I'm going to need you boys to work on filling pies in between waiting on customers, do you think you guys can handle that?"

JP looked a little worried as he met my gaze. I smiled, "Don't worry I'll show you how to do it; it's really fun and easy."

He sighed in relief, "Awesome, cause when I said I "helped" my mom sometimes I meant I stirred things and stuff like that."

Mom chuckled, "No worries. We won't wear you out on the first day."

JP smiled and turned his attention to a flood of cars pulling into the parking lot. "Woah, that's a lot of people!"

Mom shouted, "Battle stations men, let's sell some pastries!"

As she exited to the kitchen JP turned to me, "Your mom is so cool."

I smiled proudly, "Yes she is!"

The day was a whirlwind of customers and phone calls proving my social media campaign was a hit! Yes! JP did great keeping up with the rush. One time he even gave this little boy a cookie who was staring at them through the case, and I couldn't help imagining the whole time we were working side by side what it would be like when we're older and married. We made a great team. JP handled most of the to-go orders while I took care of the holiday pie pre-order line adding at least another hundred or more pies to our list. A few people were disappointed we didn't have any in stock but still placed orders. Here and there, mom would come out of the kitchen to help during the busiest peaks, and customers overhearing her talk about her pies made them join the pre-order line when they were done with JP.

When the rush finally subsided around noon, JP and I collapsed in a booth across from one another and let out a sigh in unison followed by a fit of giggles. "That was awesome!" he said as he closed his eyes and leaned his head back.

I mumbled with a half-smile, "It was nice to have someone with me and to talk to at the front counter."

He lazily opened one eye, "I can come back tomorrow if your mom doesn't mind. School doesn't start for me until next week and I haven't got anything else to do."

From behind the counter, mom said "Mind?" as she removed her apron then grabbed the cash from the register. "Of *course,* I don't mind. You're welcome to come back anytime as long as it's okay with your dad."

"Mom, do you really mean it?" I replied with excitement in my voice.

She grinned, "Well of course I do. JP did a great job and you two made a great couple, I mean... *team* out there today."

Somebody kill me! My cheeks seared with blush as I sank further into the booth. I locked eyes with mom who was staring at me smugly. She did it on purpose! Shame! My *own* mother threw me under the bus on the first day.

"Well boys, let's call it a day!"

I made my way out of the booth and JP grabbed my hand to help me stand, the sweet, simple act of which only transferred the heat from his hand directly to my face, making it even redder than it already was. "I'll see you tomorrow?" he offered.

I diverted my eyes and a goofy smile invaded my expression as I sighed, "Yeah."

He smiled, threw his hoodie on over his head, and walked past mom, "Thanks for letting me hang out today Mrs. Towler."

She grinned, "It's Dana, and you don't need to thank me. If anything, I should be thanking *you*. I don't know how we would have made it through today without you! Oh, here you go." Mom handed him an envelope with cash in it. "You worked six hours from 6 A.M. till noon. Eight dollars per hour, plus your share of the tips, you made seventy bucks today."

His eyes widened, "Awesome! Thank you so much for this!"

"You are most welcome, and we will see you tomorrow JP."

He tossed up a hand as he exited the bakery, "See you tomorrow!"

I moved to the window and pasted myself to the glass as I watched him cross the road to the big two-story farmhouse that sat across the street. He was so cute and tiny like me. I whined and pawed the glass. Mom came up behind me placing her hands on my shoulders. "He's a little cutie isn't he?"

I turned around and pouted, "He's *totes adorbs*. The gothic little black cherry on my Danish."

Mom giggled, "Uh-oh you've got it *bad* don't you?"

I quipped, "I want to marry him."

Mom chuckled, "Well, don't get too attached yet. Get to know him first or I could end up consoling you all over again just like after that whole Van episode."

I grinned, "Van *who*?"

Mom shook her head. "Lord help me through these teen years. Let's get out of here before you start thinking of names for your adopted children," she said as she patted my shoulders.

I grabbed my backpack and followed her out to the car. We stopped by the bank, then by GFS for the pie ingredients and boxes to put the pies in. After dropping off the supplies by the bakery, we made our way back home.

On the way home, I was lost in thoughts about JP and I was wondering if he was thinking about me too. Mom decided to start working on the pie orders very early in the morning so after a nap, mom fixed dinner, we watched Netflix, then retired to our rooms to get some shuteye. I couldn't wait to write in my diary.

Dear Diary,

Today I met a boy...

His name is JP He's the same height as me and has a lip ring. He wears all black and has the cutest black hair that swoops just over his eye. He lives with his dad across the street from the bakery.

I love the way he styles his hair without using his hand; he just shakes his head and it falls perfectly in place. Come to think of it, everything about him is perfect. From the way he laughs when I do something funny, to the inquisitive expression he gets on his face when he has a question.

When Van rejected me last year, I never thought I'd find another boy I felt so connected to but there's something special about JP Life is so funny. I know I'm only sixteen and just learning the ropes of things, but I have so much love to give and no one to give it to yet. I'm going to try and play it cool until I know if he likes me too. So, for now, we'll just call it a hopeful crush...

-Love, Jeffrey

CHAPTER FOUR
What's Eating JP?

The door slammed behind me as I stepped into the living room. Dad was lounging on the sofa checking emails. I stood in silence for a moment with my hands tucked into the pockets of my jeans. He lowered his glasses and lifted his gaze, "Hey sport, how'd things go at the bakery?"

I shrugged, "It was okay. Jeffrey's mom is really nice."

Dad nodded, "So the crush has a name?"

Dad stood and made his way to the kitchen as I rebutted, "We've only known each other one day."

Dad grinned, "It's about time you start socializing with kids your age instead of staying in that dark room of yours all the time."

I frowned, "You know I don't like kids my age. They think I'm weird and call me freak at school."

Dad crossed the room and placed his hand on my shoulder, "Well, this is a totally new school and now you have a friend you can stay close to."

I nodded and pulled the envelope from my pocket, "I made seventy dollars!"

Dad smiled, "Way to go buddy! What are you going to do with all that money?"

"I dunno. I wasn't really planning to make any money. I mostly just did it to stay busy."

Dad offered, "You should save some of that money so you boys can go on a nice date somewhere instead of blowing it."

I pursed my lips and remained silent about his suggestion. Although it was a great idea, I wasn't about to let on that I actually would take his advice on something.

He shook his head, "I know I work a lot since your mother passed but, without her income it's been a lot harder to make ends meet." I'm just trying hard to make life better for the both of us.

"I know dad."

Mom passed away a couple of years ago. Her name was Regina, but everyone called her Reg or Reggie. She was suddenly exhausted all the time, but she was such a strong-willed woman she wouldn't go to the doctor. When my dad finally convinced her to go after calling in to work a couple of days in a row (which she *never* did) we found out she had pancreatic cancer. She was gone less than a year after the diagnosis.

Silence lingered between us momentarily before dad said, "Hey, I have a great idea. How about we order some pizza and watch a movie? We haven't done that in a long time."

I felt a smile invade my cloudy expression as I replied, "Okay, you're on."

"Great," he said as he pulled up the app on his phone.

I made my way back to the living room and collapsed on the sofa with the remote. As I did, I couldn't help but notice the open tab on his browser. I craned my neck to see what it was…A *dating* website???

I bit my bottom lip and moved closer to get a better look… bisingles.com and the page was open to a profile of a good-looking guy.

*Oh my God! My dad is bi AND he's looking at **men**? But why hasn't he ever told me? Is he looking for a replacement for mom? Is he lonely or...just curious?* SO many questions were circling around in my head...

I could hear him coming around the corner and tried to pretend I didn't see anything. He cleared his throat and quickly closed his laptop. Then he sat down next to me and patted my leg, "So, what do you want to watch?"

I was a little weirded out by the fact my dad apparently liked women *and* men and a little angry that he never shared this with me. Was this something new or had it always been a thing? It would definitely explain why he was so accepting of me when I came out. I'll never forget that night. It hadn't been long after mom passed, and I was starting to get in trouble at school.

It all started with a phone call from my gym teacher to my dad to let him know I had been caught spying on the other boys as they were changing for practice after school. I usually hid in one of the equipment rooms, but coach caught me one day when he needed something from the closet and found me in a less than flattering position.

Thinking back, dad seemed so nervous as he sat across from me at the dining room table and said, "Son, we need to talk about what happened today."

I couldn't look him in the eyes as he explained all the general crap about how it's natural for a boy my age to be curious and have urges, but, that I just couldn't go around watching other dudes getting undressed.

To make a long story short, he ended up telling me that he loved me regardless of whether I was gay or straight, but I couldn't go around spying on people. I promised him I wouldn't do it again. I couldn't even if I wanted to because all the jocks at school started calling me *fag-*

got and trying to beat me up every time I walked into the locker room. Which is partly why we moved to Indiana and why I had to start over at a new school.

That, plus the fact that our old house (just over the state line in Kentucky) was way too big for just the two of us. When we moved here just over a week ago, I didn't expect anything to be different but by some weird twist of fate, we ended up buying a house right across the street from a nice single lady with a cute gay son.

Something twisted inside of me kind of wished Jeffrey's mom and my dad would start dating. I'd always had weird fantasies about having a brother, but we won't discuss them at this moment, besides, the thought of Jeffrey being my boyfriend is way more appealing right now than any secret desires for a taboo brocest relationship possibly coming true. *Don't look at me like that.* I *know* you've read those books out there about stepbrothers and other risky topics.

Anyways, it looks like that fantasy might be a failure before it could even get started. I mean, until I talk to dad, I don't even know what he prefers more, guys or girls. I've always liked to think I'm a pretty good judge of character. All I really want is for my dad to be happy, he really deserves it. However, I will draw the line if he likes younger guys and some dude around my age takes to calling him "daddy". *Ugh…* that would just be *too* weird.

But hey, I'm still open-minded! Maybe I *should* still try to push dad in Dana's direction? They might actually hit it off. I'm getting *way* ahead of myself…

I'm just going to eat pizza for now, zone out, and watch TV with him. I'll have to figure out a way to confront this whole "bi situation" some other time. Oh great… if he prefers *guys* over girls does that mean I have to worry about him checking out my boyfriends? *Ugh! Totally* didn't think about that.

Even with the earlier weirdness, the evening went by without a hitch. We watched *Edward Scissorhands*, my favorite movie, and chowed down on pizza like two single college frat guys so it was still pretty cool. I've missed these moments where dad and I would just *hang*. It's been pretty nice growing up with someone I could actually talk to about boys or when things got weird with my body. Initially, he *was* a little nervous, but he would always answer my questions calmly and without judgment.

After we said goodnight, I made my way upstairs to my room and turned on my music. Music is my life. It's the place where I can get lost in my thoughts and explore new worlds. I like old music from the '90s because it's all my mom and dad ever listened to while I was growing up. Yeah, I know it's not that old, but it is to me. Keep in mind, I'm only sixteen. She always called me "her little wallflower". I knew from a young age I was different. When I would mention this to my mom and she would say labels were for pickle jars and that love is love whether it's with a boy or a girl.

I've been thinking about her a lot lately. I wanted to tell her all about Jeffrey today when I got home, but I forget sometimes that she's gone. That's why I keep a journal. It makes me feel closer to her. Whenever I have a bad day, I write her a letter and by the time I'm finished, I feel a lot better.

My parents were pretty young when they had me. Mom was only 19 and my dad was 20. Despite having a kid so young, I never saw it affect their relationship and never once saw them argue or fight. They were just like two best friends who happened to live together. They always seemed to have this cool vibe and could figure out any problem together. I guess this makes sense since Mom told me they were best friends in high school. When she died, dad was devastated. He said mom was "his little black balloon in a blue sky" and the first time he saw her, he had this overwhelming need to protect her.

He said she was an "enigma". Lots of other boys tried to date her but they were all too flashy for her. She wanted a simple guy who understood when she needed space. I'm just like her that way. I want a boy who can embrace my darker side. I'm like a widow. Until the day I find the right boy, I will be in mourning. My outer look is a representation of my soul and until I find the one who will be the sun in my own sky I won't change.

I changed into my PJ's then took a seat at my desk. Today was an interesting one for sure. I only wished she were in here person for me to tell.

Dear Journal/Mom

Today I met a boy...

His name is Jeffrey. His mom owns the bakery across from our new house. (They have the best cream-filled Long Johns ever.) He's little like me and has the cutest fluffy brown hair. He wears bright colors and blue jeans and like a moth to a flame, I find myself drawn to his light and warmth.

He does the cutest things. Like, when I asked his mom if she minds if I help them out, I made the comment that I was all theirs for the day. He fainted. Literally! I said it again on purpose just to see if it was a fluke. It wasn't! A boy actually fainted over ME! He was so pretty when he was out of it, I just wanted to kiss him right then and there!

The day was full of awkward side glances and hand brushes. I know... "fangirl scream" right? I can't say yet where this will go so for now, we'll just say we're "crushing hard". I love you. I miss you. Goodnight.

-Your Little Wallflower.
JP

CHAPTER FIVE
Manic Monday

    The sound of the alarm echoed through my bedroom like a tornado siren through a tiny town. I opened my eyes and stared at the ceiling for a minute before silencing it. I really didn't want to wake up just yet, I was right in the middle of a dream about baking with Jeffrey. We had gotten into a flour fight and I was just about to kiss him when the alarm went off.
    My very first thought was how I couldn't wait to get ready and see him. Today is dad's first day at work. I lazily scratched my butt cheek as I made my way down the hall to the bathroom. I peed, stripped off my PJ's, and stepped into the shower.
    Inside the shower, I was lost in thoughts of Jeffrey again. I gently massaged my chest as I thought about him and realized I was getting really turned on. I was thinking about the way his lips looked so red and juicy like a cherry and how I wanted to nibble and suck them so bad.
    Katy Perry sang *Teenage Dream* as I got dressed. The day felt different. I felt bright and... *happy* for the first time in a long time and before long, I found myself dancing and singing into my comb. Dad opened the door and grinned. I wasn't embarrassed. We have no shame.
He even joined in. First time it's happened in a long time and I have to admit, it was pretty fun. When mom was

alive, we would sing together on family road trips and karaoke nights. After mom died, dad stopped singing and listening to music in general. He said all the songs made him sad now that he had no one to sing badly with. It hurt so much because inside I thought; *Me! You can sing badly with me Dad. I'm still here!*

The day was overcast and chilly. As I sat in our front window anxiously waiting for my sunshine to arrive and open up shop, the cloudy gray sky slowly turned the cloud cover pink as the sun began to rise behind our house which faces west toward the bakery. My tummy decided to bitch at me hard for passing up my dad's offer of oatmeal (or whatever other healthy crap he was eating) but I didn't want to get up to grab anything and possibly miss Jeffrey's arrival. If happy, geeky, goofy, awkward, and cheerful had a face it would be Jeffrey. Well… technically it does because that's what he is. He makes me laugh and feel all warm and gooey inside. Yesterday, he kept bumping into walls, tables, doors, and everything. Each time he does he shouts, "I'm okay!" I think is a regular habit of his at this point.

I had momentarily glanced away as I kept spiraling into a heart-shaped black hole inside my mind. I shook my head and placed my hands on the window as I saw them pull up across the street. I see their car over there sometimes super early in the morning but I think it's just Dana getting there to prep and bake. Over the past couple of days, I've noticed her leaving alone, then when she returns she has Jeffrey with her. I sprang into, action: pulled on my hoodie, grabbed my backpack, stepped outside, and locked the door behind me.

There was no traffic so I sprinted across the road shouting, "Jeffrey! Mrs. D.! I mean… Dana! Wait up!"

They turned around. Mrs. D... *Dana* smiled and I saw Jeffrey's eyes light up upon seeing me.

He held open his arms and shouted, "JP!"

Without thinking I ran to him, wrapped my arms around his tiny body, and lifted him off the ground. He wrapped his arms around my neck and giggled. There was an awkward pause for a minute before I sat him down. We both crossed our legs and diverted our eyes to the ground.

He traced the pavement for a minute with his foot and mumbled in a quieter tone, "I mean, Hi JP."

I ran my hand across the back of my neck and squeaked, "Hi."

Oh God. What was that sound? Was that me? Did I make that sound? Ugh. So weird... when we finally lifted our eyes from the ground, his mom was watching us with an amused expression (through the shop window) "Don't you boys skip affection on my account. I think you two are adorable." We could hear her say from inside as she turned to go back to her work.

Jeffrey turned his gaze to the sky and whispered, "Why God why?"

When he diverted his eyes back to me, I met his gaze and smiled. He rubbed his elbow nervously and said, "I'm so sorry about my mom. I mean, I hope she didn't impose a label on you or anything that is, in case you're not gay. I mean I'm gay and it's cool if you're not..."

His words trailed off as I stared at him in silence. He cleared his throat and muttered. "Kind of chilly out here."

"A little." I smiled at him.

"But I like the cold."

"Me too!" He shouted a little louder than he intended to.

His hands folded to his mouth. "I'm so sorry, that was

really loud."

His eyes were so wide and full of wonder. He looked so afraid of what I was going to say. But I was having my own problems… he's so beautiful and when I get nervous I can't speak. My heart was thumping with joy. He's the opposite; he feels the need to fill the silence with chatter. He opened his lips to speak again and I placed my hand over them.

His eyes glanced at my hand then met mine as I said, "Yes, I'm gay. Yes, it's chilly out here."

I removed my hand and his lips formed a huge smile. He opened his lips to speak again and I placed my hand back over them. His eyes widened as I said, "You don't have to keep talking, I like you… okay? But let's spend the week getting to know about each other before we put a label on anything."

He nodded in silence then I grabbed his hand before leading him inside where his mom was loading a tray of chocolate chip cookies into the front case. "I was starting to wonder if you boys were ever coming inside."

We sat our backpacks in a nearby booth, claiming our spot for when we got the chance to sit down. Jeffrey made his way behind the counter and put on his apron. His mom noticed and ran to her carry bag, "That reminds me I brought something for you JP."

"Really?" I replied curiously.

She pulled a new apron from inside her bag and tossed it to me, "Now, it's official. Welcome to the Dana's Delicious Danishes family."

I smiled and ran my fingers over the logo as I asked, "Why is it called Dana's Delicious Danishes if you serve other things as well?"

Mom rolled her eyes and chuckled, "An unfortunate oversight on my part."

Jeffrey chimed in, "Originally, we only served Danishes but we added more things over time to maximize profits."

"Ah," I replied.

I slipped it on, turned around, and asked Jeffrey with a smile, "How do I look?"

He smirked, "Like someone tried to add color to a black and white movie."

We shared a laugh and proceeded with the morning routine. After getting the coffee going and wiping the tables and booths down, his mom decided to show us how to help her with the pies. It was mostly spooning the filling into premade pie crusts. By the time the rush arrived around 9 A.M. we had already managed to fill around a hundred pies much to his mom's approval.

As the day progressed, the phone rang non-stop with more pie orders and it was sort of overwhelming, feeling like every step we took forward we got pushed two steps back. But I found I was having so much fun getting to know Jeffrey better that the work didn't even matter. In between his taking the pie orders and my pouring coffees and putting Danishes and doughnuts in bags for customers, he told me all about his dad and how he served the country and about how his mom said he was the only guy for her. I guess that puts a damper on my plan to get my dad and her to go out on a date. Before we knew it, the morning rush was over and lunchtime had crept upon us.

Jeffrey's mom emerged from the kitchen and sighed, "I'm pooped but I have to go pick up some more Pecans for the Pecan Pies, will you boys be alright here for a little bit?"

Jeffrey froze and stared blankly out the window. I grinned and replied, "We've got this… *Dana*."

I decided to make a move and put my arm around him,

"Right Jeffie?"

His face twitched and he turned his gaze to me. We held one another's gaze for a moment with a blank expression. He swallowed hard and muttered, "Yeah, we're okay."

"Good, see you guys in a bit."

As she exited and made her way to the car, Jeffrey and I continued staring at one another. I tilted my head to the side, "Your eyes are so pretty."

He closed them, smiled, and turned his head to the side. A soft chuckle vibrated through his chest and out his nose. "Thanks."

He opened them and met my gaze, "Do you really think so?"

I lifted my hand and pushed it through his hair. It was so soft, just the way I thought it would be… as soft as a kitten's tummy. I poised my hand on the back of his neck, bit my bottom lip, and whispered, "Have you ever kissed anyone?"

"No," he shook his head.

"You?"

I shook my head.

I'm so afraid, where do I go from here? His lips looked hungry. They were slightly open like he wanted to say something, but no words would come out. The sound of the front door opening prompted us to jump and I withdrew my hand. I crossed my legs and rubbed my elbow as Jeffrey tended to the customer with yet another pie order.

After taking care of the lady and ringing her up, he stood by the register staring out the window after she left. I came up behind him and playfully punched his arm. "You okay?"

He nodded in silence and went back to working on filling pies. I followed his lead and we continued working in awkward silence until his mom came back. I kept telling myself everything was okay. We just weren't ready to go there yet.

Plus, I didn't want to force him into anything too soon and ruin the beautiful friendship that was budding between us. My mom once told me that you have to earn the moments with someone you love and not try to force things to happen, just let them happen when it's the right time for them to.

There was a boy at my old school I had feelings for. His name was Rocky. We had been in the same classes since elementary school but when we got to junior high something changed between us. When puberty hit him, he got really tall, grew a mustache and his voice got really deep. He said he still felt like a little boy inside, but he felt like his body was betraying him. Growing pains... *sigh*.

It was after school and we were walking home together since his house was just up the street from mine. I remember sitting with him on the porch swing, just listening to the leaves in the tree's sing. It was early spring, and the warmth of the sun had finally started to thaw the Earth. The wind still had a chill to it. I shivered, and he wrapped his arm around me. Before either of us knew what was happening our faces were edging closer together by the second. But before Rocky could kiss me his dad pulled up and bolted from the car. I remember him shouting, "What the hell are you boys doing?"

He pulled Rocky up by his jacket collar and pushed him into the house then he told me to go on home and stay away from his son. I never talked to him again. Sure, we'd see each other around school but we never spoke again.

As time passed, I saw him hanging out more with girls. A few times I would gaze into his eyes as we passed in the hallway trying to figure out what was going on inside of his mind but he would just turn away. I could see the hurt that resided deep inside of him, the pain of his unresolved desires and emotions.

I vowed never to be that person. I want to be free. Free to love who I want, free to live the life I want without fear of judgment and I'll get it no matter what I have to do. Thankfully, I've never had to take extreme measures because my folks were always so supportive.

But now, I have these stirrings and emotions. I'm not sure how much longer I can keep them inside of me before they come erupting out like a volcano.

At the end of the day, we had managed to make almost two hundred pies. At 3:00 P.M. my dad came into the bakery and shouted, "Hiya boys what's up?"

I was so happy to see him. The afternoon had been filled with tension after what happened earlier. I wasn't sure whether he was upset we didn't get to kiss or that I'd tried too soon. Either way, I needed time to think and reassess things. I smiled at dad and said, "Dad, this is Jeffrey."

Jeffrey extended his hand with a smile and I continued, "Jeffrey, this is my dad Roger."

Dana emerged from the kitchen with a smile, "Oh, hi there again. You were here this past weekend with JP."

He extended his hand, "Yeah, I'm Roger."

Dana blushed as dad took her hand and kissed it. She held her breath and her eyes widened at his gesture and as they both withdrew. After a brief pause, she managed to say, "I'm Dana, Jeffrey's mom."

It was kind of sickening watching their exchange and I couldn't help but wonder if Jeffrey and I were that cheesy when we met. Jeffrey excused himself to go sit in our booth and gather his things. I followed him while Dana and dad chatted for a moment about mundane things like the weather. I started zoning out when dad started pretending like he understood what Dana was saying about making sure the ingredients of a pie have the right ratio.

I took the opportunity to make sure Jeffrey and I were okay. As I slipped into the booth across from him, I mumbled, "Hey."

He smiled, "Hey."

Silence lingered for a moment before I asked, "Is everything okay with us?"

He reached out his hand, placing it on top of mine and taking me surprise. His lips formed a smile, "Yes, honestly. Look JP the last boy I really liked rejected me hard so I don't want to move too fast. Does that make sense?"

I exhaled a sigh of relief, "Oh good, I thought I had done something wrong."

He looked sentimental for a moment, "Not at all. In fact, you're doing everything just right. Don't think for a second I didn't want to throw caution to the wind and kiss you until the sun sets."

I crossed my legs at the exciting thought of kissing him as it got dark outside. He continued, "For right now, let's just enjoy the ride and see where it takes us, okay?"

I nodded yes and hesitated for a moment before I replied, "Can we at least hold hands and stuff?"

Jeffrey smiled and squeezed mine, "I would like that."

Across the bakery, my dad and his mom were still chatting. Jeffrey whispered, "What do you think they're talking about?"

I arched my brow, "If I know my dad, he's putting the moves on your mom."

Jeffrey looked horrified, "Yuck!"

I giggled, "He's painful to watch. All he knows is dad

jokes and he was lucky to get mom to laugh at those when she was alive."

Jeffrey got an amused glint in his eye, "That is too funny. Can you imagine if your dad and my mom started dating and fell in love?"

I laughed nervously and wondered for a brief moment if he had been reading my journal. He was practically doubled over as he said, "And if they got married that would make us stepbrothers!"

I laughed strangely prompting him to contort his face and quip, "What was that?"

I pursed my lips then grinned, "A laugh?"

He shook his head, "You're so weird."

I lowered my gaze. It felt like cupid had aimed his arrow at me and somehow it missed. He could sense something was amiss and squeezed my hand, "Don't be sad, I'm weird too so we can just be two matching halves of a whole weirdo."

We shared another laugh before Dad and Dana came walking over to our table. Dad asked, "What are you two giggling so much about."

Jeffrey sank down in our booth, "Nothing, just weird stuff."

Dana rolled her eyes, "That's my boy. If it's odd or strange I know he will love it."

I smiled at her comment. Dad chuckled, "Sounds like you JP."

I glared at him. It was rare for my dad to embarrass me but he had actually just managed to do it. Jeffrey hid an amused smile behind his hand as his mom said, "Well, let's call it a day for today. Tomorrow is another busy day of making pies."

She turned to my dad, "Oh that reminds me, do you

guys have anywhere to go for Thanksgiving? You are more than welcome to join Jeffrey and me."

I jumped up, "Can we dad?"

He grinned, "We'll see. If your grandparents don't want us to come, I was thinking we'd probably just go to Denny's or something."

Dana waved in dismissal, "Oh, I wouldn't hear of it. You boys will join us and I'll show you how real food actually tastes."

Dad replied, "Thank you so much, Dana, that is awfully generous of you."

Turning his attention to me he said, "Ready to go home JP?"

I nodded, grabbed my backpack, and smiled at Jeffrey, "See you tomorrow?"

"See you tomorrow."

CHAPTER SIX
Something's Cooking

As I watched JP. and his dad leave, mom sank into the booth across from me and sighed. I smirked, "So, what did Roger have to say?"

She smiled a funny kind of smile I haven't seen in a while and sighed, "Well, I must say he is pretty charming and sexy. I can see where JP gets his looks from."

I smiled at the thought of JP. and my heart starting thumping like one of those little monkeys with cymbals. Mom continued, "He asked me out on a date."

I jumped, "What did you say?"

She shook her head, "Not interested. He's too starchy for me, plus, there's just something slightly off about him that I can't quite put my finger on."

Part of me was relieved but I still felt the need to ask, "But why? You said yourself he was nice looking."

Mom leaned in and covered my hand, "There is something important you need to learn. Don't go with a guy just because he's good looking. Follow your heart and not your eyes."

She wagged a finger at me and continued, "You want to know something funny?"

I tilted my head, "What?"

She giggled, "The first time I saw your father, may he rest in peace, I thought he was a meathead and wanted nothing to do with him. He was into weightlifting and on the track team."

"No way!" I shouted.

She nodded yes, "He persisted. Everywhere I would go somehow, he would always be there too and after I agreed to a date with him I found out he was really smart, funny, all that good stuff."

I smiled, "JP is really weird and makes me feel like I'm going crazy when he gets close to me. He says the oddest things at the oddest moments, and they are so funny."

Mom mumbled, "Uh-oh, sounds like you're catching the bug."

"What bug?" I quipped.

"The love bug!" She shouted as she stood and started tickling me.

Once I had regained my composure, I bit my bottom lip and whispered, "He almost kissed me today."

Mom arched her brow as I packed my things and we made our way to the door. Once we were in the car, she turned to me, "Did you?"

I sighed as I gazed out the window, "It felt too soon."

She nodded, "Did you feel anything before it almost happened?"

I turned to her, "Like my soul was about to leave my body and he was the one taking it."

We made our way to the car, and once we were inside mom sighed, "Uh-oh."

"What?" I quipped.

"You've already caught it."

"The love bug," I smirked.

"Yep, it'll happen soon just be careful."

"Be careful?"

"As I said, listen to your heart, not your winkie."

Oh, dear Lord! Please tell me my mother did not just say the word winkie! Can I open the car door and take my chances? I would have if we wouldn't have already been en route to the house.

"Ma, *please!*" I shouted.

She giggled, "Well, it's true, and you're a boy. Sometimes guys think with their head down there instead of the one above the waistline."

I whined, "I would really rather not talk about this right now."

"Suit yourself, but I'm here if you have any questions."

It was nearly 4:00 P.M. when we got home and I couldn't wait to take a nap. My dreams were filled with fantasies of JP as usual, which only added to the parade of emotions I was feeling about him. The evening was pretty uneventful. We ate dinner at home, watched some TV, then said goodnight. These long days always take all of our energy but, we were well on track to making enough money to pay up the bills for a while.

As I prepared for bed an IG message came through from JP. I slid open my screen to find he had sent me a picture of himself... in bed! I held the phone to my chest. My heart was flopping like a sandal caught in a lawnmower.

I slowly pulled the phone away from my chest to find him wearing a faded My Chemical Romance t-shirt with his belly button showing, hair was a mess and in his boxers. *Drool!* The message read, *"Just wanted to say good night...and say I'll be thinking about you."*

I kept the picture open and rushed to my diary...

Dear Diary,
Today I almost had my first kiss with JP. We were inter-

rupted before we could do anything. Newsflash, he sent me a goodnight text. I've never received a goodnight text and I'll cherish it forever.

He's not like other boys, he's quiet and weird and just Gah! I don't know what to say! For the first time in my life, I'm speechless. I'm going to go snuggle with my phone and think about him… with any luck, twice.

XOXO-Jeffrey

Before I laid down to sleep, I decided to send him a reply. I was lying on my tummy with my feet in the air. I tried my best to look cute. *Send!*

A reply came in, *"You're so adorable and I can't wait to see you tomorrow."*

I let out a sigh and a smile formed on my lips as I stared at the picture he sent me and my hand drifted lower. Before long I had fallen asleep…

In the morning I woke up with a huge smile and another text that said, "*Good morning.*"

I bit my bottom lip and replied, "Good morning, can't wait to see you."

"Winking emoji. *Same.*"

After a shower, a cherry Danish, and a quick gathering of my things, I was out the door and on my way to meet mom at the shop. Something felt off today as I approached the bakery. I kept glancing at the house across the street expecting to see JP rush out and over at any moment but he never did. I waited around a while but he never came. Mom could tell I was upset as I tucked my thumbs into the straps of my backpack, lowered my head, and finally made my way inside. "Maybe he just overslept?" she offered as she came out from the kitchen covered in various ingredients and attempting to push a stray lock of hair back without getting any on it.

I tried to text him, but my message was left unseen and after an hour of frequently checking there was no response. I couldn't help but wonder if I had said or done something wrong and those wonderings affected my performance all day. Someone save me from myself!

It started when I burned myself on the coffee machine, then while trying to fill a box of doughnuts I dropped them on the floor. If that weren't bad enough, I kept writing people's credit card numbers down incorrectly and would have to call them back to have them read it to me again. Just for references, people don't like that very much.

To say I was thankful when lunchtime came was an understatement. I was beyond ready to go home and pretend this day *never* happened.

Part of me hoped so desperately JP would come rushing in at the last moment like they do in the movies and make everything okay by saving the day, but he didn't. So, I sulked and got lost in my music as I cleaned up the bakery and waited for mom to finish what she needed before we went home.

On the ride home, mom kept trying to reassure me that everything was okay, but I wasn't in the mood to hear it. "Baby, he probably had to run errands with his dad or something important; they did just move to town."

I mumbled, "Yeah, sure, whatever," as I opened the screen door and sauntered to the front porch. My disappointment had turned into anger. I didn't even bother to change my clothes; I just collapsed in bed and buried my head under the covers. Thank God it's winter, which will just make this day end quicker.

When I awoke, it was late in the evening around dinner. I didn't want anything to eat but mom fixed me a TV dinner and forced me. I was still sulking from JP ignoring my messages all day and I didn't even bother to check the phone until much later. He had tried to get in touch with me over and over again. I couldn't help but feel like a brat for thinking all the bad things I had throughout the day. At one point I had even convinced myself that love didn't exist and boys sucked and not in the good way. I'd just be single and watch porn if I was feeling romantic, at least boys in a video couldn't hurt me. There was no emotion behind it.

His message read, *"Jeffrey, I am so sorry for blowing you off today but we had the closing on our old house, and dad forced me to go. He said he needed my help. It took all day and I swear I wasn't ignoring you."*

Maybe I overreacted earlier? Okay geez! Fine, I totally overreacted but you know what you're a judge-a-roo; so there! Darn it, you can't see me sticking my tongue out at you. Um, should I apologize back?... But he doesn't know I was mad at him!... Okay fine, there's no need to get huffy about it!

I replied, *"It's okay. I'm sorry for not replying sooner, I was a little pissed off, but I was mostly worried I had done something wrong."*

He sent a rolling eyes emoji, *"Newsflash, just because someone can't talk doesn't mean they are mad at you. Insecure much?"*

I was smiling as I fired back, *"Um, you don't know me well enough yet to be able to read my emotions that well; are you psychic or something?"*

He sent me a clever looking smiling emoji, *"I get a psy-kick out of you."*

"Soooo cheesy," I replied.

He texted me a selfie of him with a stuffed wedge of cheese. *Dead! Officially! Call the undertaker! I'm so going to marry this boy one day...*

Silence lingered for a few minutes before he replied, "*I'm really tired so I'm going to go to bed but I promise I will be at the bakery bright and early so we can hand out all those pie orders.*"

"*Okay, goodnight.*"

"*Goodnight, babe.*"

I was lying on my back in bed and dropped the phone on my face. Ouch! Don't you hate when that happens? Huh, wait...did he just call me babe? He called me babe! *O.M.G!*

Dear Diary,
   Today he called me "babe" ... that is all.

Love, Jeffrey

CHAPTER SEVEN
Crush…Rush

The day before Thanksgiving. Somehow, we pulled it off. Yesterday mom and I finished up all the pie orders and today is the day where everyone comes to pick them up. We barely had enough time to eat breakfast. We got ready in a rush; it was just a sign of how busy the day was going to be.

I was anxious on the way to the bakery. I craned my neck and peered out the window to see if JP was there like he said he would be. Mom turned to me and smiled, "Look who's here!"

She had barely finished the statement before I was out of the car and sprinting toward him. I could see his breath hovering in the chilly morning air. He lifted his head; his face was framed by his hoodie. The streetlamp in front of the bakery highlighted his face and he grinned, "Told you I'd be here."

I stood in front of him for a moment unsure of what to do then threw my arms around him and he reciprocated. Our first hug; it was everything and more than I thought it would be. I could feel the pressure of his arms tighten around me. As we separated, I poked his chest, "I'm still mad at you!"

He tucked his hands into his hoodie pockets and shrugged, "I said I was sorry."

My lips twitched into a grin, "Promise, even if you're busy from now on that you'll at least let me know you're okay. I was worried you were hurt or that I'd done something to upset you."

He removed one hand from his pocket and held out a pinky, "I promise."

I stared at him inquisitively before wrapping my pinky around his and we smiled. Mom passed us on the way to the door, "Glad to see you could make it today JP"

"Glad I could make it, sorry about yesterday."

She turned to him after unlocking the door, "Quite alright, but I'm afraid your unexcused absence will be going on your permanent record with the company."

JP giggled, "Fair enough."

She jerked her head, "Get in here, we've got a lot of work to do today."

We followed her inside and she clicked on the lights. After our morning set up routine of coffee making, setting up the display cases, and brings all the pie orders to the shelves behind the counter I rushed to turn on the open sign. It wasn't long before the masses descended to pick up their orders and just as we thought the day was filled with chaotic bliss. Mom even had to set JP up with a makeshift cash register to collect money.

It was nice having him back beside me. I felt lost without him yesterday and I couldn't shake the feeling that this was the new norm. He was the calm to my storm, the left to my right, the right to my wrong. After the last customer picked up her order JP and I collapsed in a nearby booth to rest while mom counted the cash and prepared it for depositing.

I hadn't even noticed we were sitting on the same side of the booth; his leg was touching mine. I was all too aware when he suddenly rested his hand on my thigh and turned to me, "That was exhausting."

I smiled, "Yes, it was. My legs hurt so bad."

He licked his lips and whispered, "I could massage them for you…that is, if you want me to."

Ah! Not now boner! I crossed my arms over my crotch in an effort to hide the excitement; he grinned at me and I realized he was in the mood to play but I changed the subject, "So, are you and your dad joining us for Thanksgiving?"

He frowned, "I wish; I have to go with dad to my grandma and grandpa's house in Louisville."

I whined, "Will we get to chat any?"

He nodded, "Yeah, I'll be texting you a lot because there is literally nothing to do there."

We shared a laugh, then silence lingered between us. Suddenly he shifted and I could feel his fingers laced with mine. I glanced down at them then back at him; he whispered, "Is that okay?"

I nodded in shocked silence and he smiled, "Good."

He went back to playing Candy Crush on his phone but my eyes were locked on him. He was holding my hand; they were so soft and a little cold. I'd always dreamed of holding a boy's hand so many times I'd fantasized about what it would feel like and just like that I was, and it was everything I dreamed it would be.

Mom grabbed her purse and coat and made her way to the door, "Alrighty, this day is done. Let's go home!"

But I didn't want to go. I could have sat there in that booth holding JP's hand forever. He lifted his eyes from his phone and looked a little sad. "Um, when do you think we can see each other again?"

I thought for a moment, "Well, there is Thanksgiving, then Black Friday mom and I always go to the sales."

"Saturday or Sunday," he said desperately.

I sighed, "I sure hope so because school starts back on Monday and I want to get to hang out with you before life gets all busy and stuff."

We stood and gathered our things as mom switched the lights off in the bakery. He walked with me to the car; mom got inside and started it while I lingered with him a little longer.

"So, I guess I'll see you in a couple of days then?"

I whimpered, "Yeah."

He and I were staring at the ground. He lifted his head and met my gaze. I couldn't help but be mesmerized by the cute way he was biting nervously at his lip ring. The tension lingering in the air around us was unbearable like the stillness before a storm. We were waiting for lightning to strike but nothing happened. He sighed, "I'll see you when I see you."

As he turned to walk home I shouted, "JP wait!"

He turned around and I rushed over to him. My lips parted then bang! It happened! I leaned in and kissed his cheek. He stood in shock for a moment and a tinge of pink highlighted his cheek as he lifted his hand slowly to touch it. I rushed to the car and sank into my seat.

Mom grinned at me, "What just happened?"

I was covering my face with my hands as she nudged me, "Come on, dish!"

I unveiled my eyes and whispered, "I just kissed JP for the first time."

Mom squealed and wrapped me in a hug, "Congratulations!"

She separated from me and shifted the car into drive, "So, how did it feel?"

I mumbled, "Like I'm a little red balloon floating aimlessly through the sky."

Mom gushed, "Aw! That is so sweet."

As we pulled away, I saw JP staring out the screen door at our car. He placed his hand on the glass of the door and I placed my hand on the window of the car. It was in that moment I knew something had changed between us, someone had struck a match inside of our hearts and it had ignited into a sweet romance. This was no longer a crush. What am I supposed to do now? I've only ever known how to crush. My affections had never been returned and now that they had been, I felt like someone had ripped my guts out and I was trying to stuff them back inside of me before I died.

So many new questions were now clouding my blue skies, but I don't have the time to figure out how to answer them right now.

JP

As I stood in the doorway to my house watching Jeffrey leave, I was numb. I'd spent endless nights longing for my first kiss and I had no idea it was going to happen like this. Now that it had I didn't know how to cope with all the emotions I was now feeling. I wanted to run after him, I wanted to go further, I just wanted…him.

I watched as dad pulled into the driveway and come to the door. He stared at me curiously as he stepped inside, "Is everything okay buddy?"

I squeaked, "Yeah."

He sighed, "On no, did something happen with you and Jeffrey."

I nodded, "But it was a good thing." I met his gaze, "How did it feel the first time you kissed mom?"

Dad flashed me a half-smile, "Like someone had just let the air out of me."

He set his briefcase down and descended to one knee then he took my hands, "Listen buddy I know you've waited for someone like Jeffrey for a long time but don't overthink things."

"It was our first kiss," I mumbled.

He smiled, "And that's great, now take that chemistry and think about your next move. Spend some time getting to know one another to make sure you both have the same goals. If it's true love, then it will find a way to be."

I nodded as he stood, and as he took his coat off, I asked, "Dad, can I talk to you about something?"

He shuffled through the mail, "Sure bud, what is it?"

I swallowed hard, "Have you ever been attracted to a boy?"

He froze and silence lingered before he asked, "Why do you ask?"

I stuttered for a moment as I said, "The other night I noticed you were looking at a dating website with guys on it."

Dad's expression turned hard, "Why were you looking at my laptop?"

I answered quickly, "It was just open and I couldn't help but notice...

My words trailed off and he growled, "They have both guys and girls and I was just looking. It just happened to be on guys."

He was becoming increasingly nervous. I watched as he shifted swiftly through the mail then he growled, "Look, son, I'm not looking for anyone right now."

I approached him and rested my hand on the stair rail, "Dad it's okay if you're curious. In fact, there are so many questions I have for you if you think you might like guys."

Dad growled, "Son, I just got off work and I don't want to talk about this right now."

I shouted, "Just when I think we have something in common you prove me wrong. Mom's gone and I have so many emotions right now that I don't know how to deal with, but I guess it's too much to expect my dad to be honest with me."

Dad froze and as I turned to run up the stairs as he shouted, "JP wait!"

The door slammed behind me as I dove onto my bed, burying my face into my pillow. A few minutes later a knock came at the door, "Son, can I come in?"

I didn't answer, but he came in anyway. I turned to face the wall and I could feel him sit down at the end of the bed. He sighed, "Look, son, I had a few minor crushes on guys but then met your mom and that was it. I don't have any experience to be able to tell you what you need to know about being with guys."

I mumbled a reply, "Mom would've known what to say."

"Well mom's gone and I'm too scared of what you might ask me." He barked.

I turned to him, "Sometimes all I need is for someone to listen and not say anything."

He swallowed hard and whispered, "I'm sorry."

I started to cry, "I really like Jeffrey a lot but what's going to happen when school starts, and we have our own lives to live and can't be together all the time. I just need to know that this isn't some kind of crush. I need more than that. I have urges and I can't bear watching all the couples at school while I'm still alone."

Dad stared at me empathetically, "How do you think I feel? I didn't expect your mother to die. I had planned to spend the rest of my life with her."

I listened as he stood and paced, "I hate being alone. It isn't easy living on your own. Every time one of my co-workers gets a phone call from their spouse or when I see couples eating their lunch together at a restaurant, I miss your mom."

I whispered, "But you're not alone. I'm right here and I've been here all along."

Dad froze again, "Oh son, I didn't mean to make it sound like I...um...that you..."

I rose up, "I know you didn't mean to, but you did."

He closed his eyes and lowered his head, "I'm sorry. I'm just so lost with this new job, in this new town, and this new house. Everything is just so new, and I don't cope well with change."

I shook my head, "Well neither do I but mom always said if you make a decision just stick to it and whether things turn out good or bad you can always make another decision to fix it."

Silence lingered between us before I continued, "So if you want to go on a date with a guy then do it. If you don't like it, then at least you tried, but I really need your advice. I don't want to miss a chance at something wonderful with Jeffrey once fall break is over."

Dad looked wise for a moment, "Well son, I'm going to be honest with you. Sometimes life gets in the way of things you really want to do, they're called priorities and if you really want to make things work with Jeffrey then you're going to have to find the time to spend with him."

Dad shifted to the top of my bed and laid down with his hands behind his head, "Now, why don't you tell me what happened that brought up all of these emotions."

I smiled, "Well today was super busy at the bakery and when everything was done, Jeffrey and I sat next to each other in a booth and we held hands for the first time. It just felt so right."

"And?" dad said.

"Well, as we were leaving, we kind of just stared at the ground for a minute like we were waiting for something to happen. It was so weird."

"Then what happened?"

My lips twitched and I tried to suppress an oncoming grin, but I couldn't help it. "Then, as I was turning to go home he shouted my name and he kissed me on the cheek."

Dad turned to me and rested his hand on the side of his head, "It sounds like you boys shared your first special moment."

I replied, "Yeah, but did he kiss me because of the tension or because he felt like he had to?"

Dad chuckled, "If he called you back, he was waiting for you to kiss him, but when you didn't, he decided to. Why didn't you kiss him first?"

"I was too scared to!" I whined.

Dad exhaled, "Bud, it's okay to be afraid. That's how it always feels before a first kiss."

I mumbled as I stared up at the ceiling, "It was so awesome!"

Dad mumbled, "Then you did it right."

He stood and made his way to the door, "Falling in love is like a roller coaster ride. It's scary as you're making that initial climb, then when you get to the top it's terrifying. But, once you've reached the top there is no changing your mind, you just have to let go and hope for the best. Does that make sense bud?"

"Uh-huh," I nodded. Before I knew it the rush of the day had caught up with me and I succumbed to sleep with new hope that even though we were going to be apart for a couple of days if what we have is meant to be then it will be. One thing is for sure like dad said, there's no turning back now. I'm just going to have to let go and whatever happens, will happen."

Later that night, I woke and found dad on the couch with his laptop. "Whatcha doin?" I asked.

He smirked, "Our talk earlier prompted me to take a chance of my own."

I rushed over to him, "Are you talking to guys?"

"Maybe," he said.

I smiled, "Any cute ones?"

He looked embarrassed, "Most of them are so young and I'm old enough to be their dad."

I plopped down beside him, "That's a thing in the community you know?"

He looked intrigued for a moment, "It is…wait how do you know?"

I looked away nervously, "I um…I…"

After a few painful moments, I finally managed to say, "There are lots of younger guys who like to date older guys."

He closed his eyes, shook his head, then closed his laptop, before standing up. "Why don't we order some dinner?"

"Okay," I said as he grabbed a stack of takeout menus off the coffee table. We ended up ordering Chinese takeout and chatting for hours. He really opened up about the urges he felt. He explained how he had always liked guys but back when he and mom met, he was scared to pursue those desires. He also admitted he is bi and when he falls in love, he falls in love with someone's personality not just their physical attributes. It was the first time we had *really* connected since mom was alive and it felt so good to have a dad again.

But, for all the good things that happened today, I still couldn't help but feel a little sad for him. I'd found a way to deal with some of my emotions by writing my thoughts and feelings in the form of letters to my journal/mom but all this time I'd forgot to check on dad to see how he was holding up; boys get sad too you know?

Dear Journal/Mom

Today I learned something,

Today I kissed a boy and it left me with all of these new emotions. As things get more serious with Jeffrey, I started to grow afraid of losing him. It's like going for a walk and finding a really pretty rock, so you tuck it away in your pocket so you don't lose it. But I started to worry so much that there was a hole in my pocket that I lost the joy of the moment in finding this new, really pretty thing.

I got so caught up worrying about where our relationship was going and if we'd still be able to stay as close as we are now when school starts that I didn't even get to bask in the joy of my first real kiss. I mean, I've kissed a boy before but kissing Rocky was different; it was just an experiment that I never got to see the results of because his dad refused to let his son explore his urges.

Tonight, I'm so thankful dad is such an open-minded guy; oh, did you know he is bi? We had an argument today because I found him looking at dating websites with guys on them. It's funny really, he's kind of going through the same emotions I am right now; unsure of what to do or how to pursue a relationship. I wish you were here to help him through this but, then again, if you were still here then he wouldn't be looking at other guys to date then anyways would he?

Tonight, we talked for hours and I suggested that he write you a letter, just like I do and he really looked like he was thinking about doing it so maybe you'll hear from him soon? I have to go text Jeffrey.

-Hugs & kisses from your little wallflower, JP.

CHAPTER EIGHT
What's Eating Roger

After JP and I said goodnight I stayed up for a little while longer; cleaned up the house a little bit after dinner, then retired to my room. I've never been much of a housekeeper, but I do my best. You can just imagine with two guys living together the house gets a little unkempt to say the least. I know we haven't been formally introduced yet but I'm Roger, nice to meet you.

Lately, I've been thinking a lot about life. What do you do when all your plans for life go up in smoke? When I figure out the answer to that question, I'll let you know. I've always believed that everything happens for a reason, that's how we ended up here in Indiana. It wasn't a far move, just over the river from Kentucky but the symbolism behind the move is what's important. JP and I needed a fresh start.

He'd been getting bullied a lot at his old school as I'm sure he's already told you all about. He expresses himself better on paper than in person so you should be happy he actually even talks to you. Until tonight, we hadn't had a normal conversation in years. He reminds me so much of myself at that age; lost, lonely, and trying to figure himself out. I guess we all go through that as teenagers. I could sit here and pretend like JP's problems were the only reason we moved but I had reasons of my own.

The truth is, I needed to break free from the rut I was in. I'd been working the same dead-end job at an investment firm for years. Living in the same house I bought with my wife, Regina, years before JP was born and driving the same car I'd been driving since high school. I guess you could say I was one of those responsible kids.

I can thank my parents for that. They were overachievers in every definition of the word. My dad was a Navy chief before he retired, and he ran a tight ship at work and at home. Mom was a district manager for a fast-food chain and a homemaker. As an only child, I had a great childhood. My parents raised me with good morals and a strong work ethic; and those factors made me the man I am today.

Reggie was the total opposite of myself. She was in and out of foster homes throughout her childhood. By the time I met her in high school, she was living with an ultra-conservative Christian family. She was a "bad girl" and I loved everything about her. She smoked, listened to heavy metal music, and rarely did anything her foster parents told her to.

The day we met; I was sitting on the sidewalk in front of school waiting for my mom to pick me up. She was walking home because she didn't live far from school and hated riding the bus. I don't know why she decided to sit down beside me. We started talking, then suddenly we found ourselves meeting every day just to sit and talk about nothing. One thing led to another and when I asked her to senior prom she said yes.

After graduation, we both got jobs and rented a small apartment in downtown Louisville. We weren't rich by any means, but we had everything we needed. She worked at a posh restaurant as a waitress in the beginning then eventually worked her way up the ranks to pastry chef while I went to college to get a degree in finance. I'd always loved math and you can pretty much say I was a nerd but, I eventually got a job as a bank loan officer which is where I worked until JP and I moved here to Indiana.

I'll never forget when we found out Reggie had cancer; she had been sick for months with extreme intestinal pain, so bad that she eventually started calling in to work all the time which is when she finally relented and allowed me to take her to go see a doctor. Turns out her strength ended up becoming her greatest downfall. I guess I'm still angry at her for pushing through the pain and pretending everything was okay. She didn't even make it a year after her diagnosis of stage four pancreatic cancer. If she hadn't been so stoic, so... *stubborn*, she'd still be here with us today.

After she died, I just couldn't stand to live in the house we shared together any longer. Everything about it reminded me of her. We bought the place not long after I got the job as a bank loan officer and she got promoted to pastry chef at the restaurant. The decision to buy a house directly coincided with the news she was pregnant with JP.

Now that we've moved, I'm having trouble adjusting to all of the changes. I feel like I did when I was a teenager all over again. Here I am, a lonely middle-aged widower raising a gay teenage boy by myself. So many years have gone by and there are so many years left and I don't know what to do with all this time. JP is all I have left of the world I used to know and until tonight I thought I'd lost him too.

I must admit I'm a little jealous that he has found someone. How can I give first crush advice to a kid whose life is just beginning when I'm still coping with the fact that mine has ended? Well, technically it hasn't ended but, right now, I kind of feel like the lone survivor of a plane crash. The memories of the life I had play over and over inside my mind but I feel so far away from the man I was in those memories.

You're probably wondering why I don't go after Jeffrey's mom Dana? I mean, she's single, I'm single why not? Well, the thing is, she is a wonderful and confident woman who has a good head on her shoulders, and I always seem to be attracted to people who are broken. I have this overwhelming need to take care of someone. Reggie needed someone. She needed someone to love her for who she was, to let her make her own decisions and if she was wrong, I was there to pick her up and tell her everything was going to be okay. Now, it seems like I'm the one needing someone to tell me everything is going to be okay and that I made the right decisions.

Maybe I'm selfish but I'm looking for someone who is going to make me feel special and needed, like a man again. Tonight during our conversation, JP told me that I might be able to reconcile my feelings by writing Reggie a letter, so, under the advice of a sixteen-year-old boy, I'm sitting here waiting for the words to come but I don't know what to say. When they come, I'll be ready but for now, I'm going to bed.

CHAPTER NINE
Back to Life

Thanksgiving was nice. Mom and I had a nice quiet dinner at home and on Black Friday JP joined us in the madness. Picture it, mom running through the mall, shopping bags stacked up her arms shouting, "Keep up boys!"

It was so much fun. I kept reaching back to grab JP's hand and when we finally got to sit down he turned to me saying, "Your mom is crazy!"

I grinned, "I know, but she's my crazy and I love her."

She gave him an extra hundred dollars bonus in addition to his pay for all of his help during what we are now calling "The Great Pie-a-Thon". We made enough money to pay up all the bills and you'll be happy to know the bakery is going to be open for a long time. Plus, with JP working with us mom won't need to call back the extra staff, except for the night baker. That way she won't have to go in so early.

School started back the following Monday and because the bus runs right by the bakery, JP and I get to ride the bus to and from school together. A few weeks have gone by without a hitch and we've been growing closer and learning more about one another every day. I think he was initially worried that we wouldn't get to spend much time together when school started but those fears were relieved after the first week or so.

Our parents even let us have sleepovers on the weekends; one week at his house, the next at mine. You'd think something would have happened between us by now, but he hasn't made a move and I'm starting to get a little desperate. I find myself intentionally posing in sexy positions and changing in front of him to stoke the fire a little bit and nothing! What am I doing wrong? I've learned that he's a very reserved person which is fine, but I'm starting to run out of ideas.

Christmas is coming and school is about to go on winter break. I can't wait, but, everything isn't as perfect as it seems. Lately, Van has started trying to talk to me again. Actually, it's more like bullying. He and his football buddies have cornered JP and me several times and thrown our books in the trash or pushed us into lockers and called us fags. My mom and his dad eventually had to sit down for a conference with the principal and Van's foster parents after they gave JP a black eye because he tried to protect me.

Sigh! He's so *dreamy*! He's so little but he's wiry and most of the time he can get away from them, but not even he could escape four big football players. Thank God our science teacher, Mrs. Pritchett was around, or they might have done worse damage than just a black eye. I wasn't aware that he had similar problems at his old school, but my heart melted when he told me all about it and said, "At least I don't have to suffer alone now."

No one had bothered me before JP, in fact, Van avoided me at all costs until he started noticing me with him. Things changed one day when he came up to me after school while I was waiting for JP to come out and asked, "Who's your new friend?"

I had no secrets from Van. He may have hurt my heart,

but he never tried to physically hurt me after I told him I liked him, so I didn't think I had any reason to hide anything from him. I told him that JP was my boyfriend and a strange expression washed over his face like something had snapped in his brain. Suddenly, he couldn't look at me, he just stared numbly ahead, rolled his jaw, and mumbled, "Oh."

The next day, he was with his buddies on the football field and shouted, "Hey boys check out the two fags on the bleachers watching us!"

They immediately turned their focus to us and began shouting, "Get the hell out of here! This is a private practice!" He met my gaze and stiffened his upper lip before turning away. Maybe he was jealous, but why would he be jealous of JP when he said himself that he wasn't gay?

VAN

It had been a while since the season ended, but the guys and I kept up our practices until it got too cold to do so. I'd rather be at school with them anyway that at my so-called house. The truth is, I'm actually waiting for them to throw me out at any second. It's the way it goes in the system.

I've been in foster care for as long as I can remember. It's no big deal. I don't need your sympathy and I've made it this far without any help from anyone so just keep your emotions in check. Sports are my escape, my escape from this so-called life, and this shithole of a town. I figure if I work hard enough maybe I can get a scholarship or something and get the hell out of here. I think my current foster rents are just letting me stay until I graduate.

I always hate this time of year, when school lets out for the holidays and everyone's busy tending to Christmas crap. I don't even celebrate it anymore. When I was little, I used to write Santa a letter asking him for a family, but that dream died a long time ago. I don't even know who my real parents are, and I don't care because they obviously didn't want me. The only person I can remember ever wanting me was Jeffrey and after today, I'm pretty sure he'll never want anything to do with me again. I don't know why I always push everyone away. I guess I figure if I don't let anyone get too close it won't hurt as bad when they throw me away the way my parents did.

Even though we're the same age, Jeffrey was always a couple of grades below me in school because I'd failed a few years which is why I'm still here. It isn't like I'm stupid or anything, I just didn't give a shit about school much until I got on the football team and had to keep my grades up. I just need to borrow time until I figure out where I'm going once my foster parents turn me out. They don't really care what I do, as long as I go to school and stay out of trouble with the law. I haven't got time to be in trouble, between work and school and football, I'm barely home at all.

I work the second shift at a local burger joint and I've been there for around a year now. I'm actually on my way there now. Sitting on the bus with my earbuds in listening to Linkin Park or something I can zone out and be just another nameless face on the way to work which It's the only peace I have. I like being alone. The only person I can depend on in this life is myself and when I listen to my music I can get lost in my thoughts and kinda fall into one of those dreams where you're dead and kind of hovering over the world, watching people as they go about their mundane lives… That's how I feel when I listen to my music and it's comforting to me.

I'll be glad when this shift is over. I've been here for nearly four hours and business is so slow. There's an older guy who works the same shift as I do who lets me relieve some of his "tension" on our breaks. He usually buys me beer or something and he's nice enough, but I don't see our relationship ever evolving to anything more than friends with benefits.

I don't live far from school so a lot of times when I get off work, I go to the football field and get drunk. It's the only place I can say I ever feel anything. When I'm on that field, I feel at home and I remember the times when Jeffrey and I used to sit and do homework. His mom makes the best damn cookies in the county. Jeffrey told me what they were called once but I can't remember now.

Back when he first started coming to this school, I remember thinking he looked and acted so different from the other boys. We actually met one day when he was waiting for the bus. I was walking down the sidewalk and dropped my earbuds; he picked them up and ran up behind me shouting, "Hey, hey! You dropped these."

I was lost reading some crap on my phone and didn't even feel them drop out of my backpack. When I turned around, there he was, standing in front of me with a nervous smile. I remember my eyes locking onto his hair; it was super fluffy like cotton candy and cute like one of those big stuffed animals from the carnival. I just wanted to touch it. If you tell anyone I said the word *cute*, I'll pound you.

Anyways, we ended up talking while he waited for his mom to pick him up. Well, he talked, and I just listened. I never know what to say in conversations and rather than look stupid I just don't say anything. It was nice communicating with another human being for once, it made me feel real, like I mattered enough for someone to waste their breath talking to me. The extent of communication with my football buds is, "Sup?" or various plays during practice or a game.

It's the same at work. The only communication I have with my coworkers is to let them know an order is up or my boss yelling at me to keep up the pace. The dude I mentioned who I hang out on break with is the sandwich maker. I'm the grill cook and if it wasn't for his jokes, the way he makes fun of our boss, and the fact that I need the money, I would have quit this job a long time ago. Fast food ain't no place for a high school kid.

My buds from school tease me for not having a girlfriend yet, but I can do bad by myself. Girls are nothing but trouble anyway, I've been with a few and they're all the same. They only want me for a trophy or someone to experiment with. Besides, I don't actually swing that way. I've never told anyone, but I really like hanging out with older guys which I guess goes back to my childhood. I always wanted a *real* dad, someone who would have taught me how to play sports, let me hand him tools while he works on his car, or just to chill with while we watch the game. Someone who made me feel special and called me dad nicknames like *kiddo*, *slugger*, or *sport*. I wanted so desperately to be somebody's boy; I still do, but now that I'm almost eighteen and getting ready to be thrown out on my ass, it kinda looks like that ship has sailed. What a glamourous life eh? A soon to be high-school graduate with no real past or future, flipping burgers to get enough money for the things I need.

It's Friday night and you'd think I'd be out with

friends; hanging out, partying, just shooting the shit like young dudes do. Sometimes I think that kind of life would be fun. It would certainly be less lonely but, then I realize I'd rather be alone than pretending I'm someone I'm not; a passing for straight jerk-off who lets his dick make his decision for him.

Sex means nothing to me; passion is life. Show me a person who makes my skin crawl with intellectual stimulus and I'll be on my knees faster than a sinner at the altar. I want to feel things far beyond the physical. Match my snark with wit then tell me all your hopes and dreams as we lie on the hood of your car and gaze up at the night sky. I want someone to whisper sweet nothings in my ear as we hold naked in the dark. Even if they're lies, no explanation is needed. I promise I'll understand that it was just the heat of the moment telling you what your heart meant.

People always say things they don't mean when they are pretending, but I'll take a night of pretending with a comfortable stranger any day as opposed to a life of boring reality filled with wannabes. I want to live my life with no regrets. If I make a decision that turns out to be a mistake, just catch me when I fall, help me to my feet, and teach me what I did wrong so I can learn from it instead of telling me what a stupid decision it was in the first place. Isn't part of the fun of being young having the freedom to live dangerously?

Speaking of living dangerously, I've been off work waiting for the last bus home for the past fifteen minutes. I managed to score a pint from my bud at work and it's starting to hit me pretty hard. I'd been hitting it hard since I sat down at the bus stop. I took another shot from my paper bag as the bus approached. It stopped and the door opened. I was having a little trouble coordinating my steps. I dropped my fare and searched for a seat. No one else was on board and the bright lights were making my head pound. I shook my head to snap myself out of it.

I remembered that the bus goes by Jeffrey's mom's bakery and noticed that his little boyfriend lives across the street...

Call me crazy but I'm feeling brave and I'm tired of being alone.

I was going to do it! I was going to do what I should've done a year ago when Jeffrey told me that he liked me but was too stupid to do at the time; I was going bare my soul and confess my true love just like boys do to girls in those cheesy 80's movies.

I could see the bakery up ahead, I signaled for my stop, and the bus began to slow. The doors opened and I stepped down. I'd been chugging hard to keep up my nerve. When I stepped down, I stumbled a little as the bus pulled away and threw my empty bottle into the nearby grass. I stripped off my uniform shirt leaving on my white wife-beater underneath then tugged my belt from the loops of my pants and drug it behind me as I approached the house where I'd once seen Jeffrey with *him* snuggled up on the front porch.

I could barely see; everything was a blur and the porch light was blinding me, but I was ready, ready to fight for the boy I... *love*? I pounded on the glass with my fist, "Jeffrey! Jeffrey!"

Nothing but silence came from inside of the house, so I pounded harder, "I know you're here with *him*! I've come to get you back! *I saw you first!*"

I pounded again, "Tell him to come out here now and fight me like a man or I'm busting down this door!"

I stood up straight and stiffened my upper lip as I heard

the door unlock and creak open. A booming voice shouted, "What the hell kid! It's 11 PM!"

I was having trouble making out faces, but I could tell it wasn't Jeffrey or JP "Who the hell are you?" I slurred.

The man crossed his arms and growled, "I'm Roger, JP's father and the boys aren't here. They're spending the weekend at Jeffrey's place."

ROGER

I felt bad and a little worried for the boy standing before me, "What's your name kid?"

"Van," he slurred.

I took a whiff, "Son, have you been drinking?"

He snapped back, "What's it to you?"

I tried to play it cool, although my fatherly instincts were out of control. "How'd you get here?"

He was still trying to keep his balance as he replied, "Calm down *grandpa*, I took the bus."

I rolled my jaw and tried to ignore the fact he called me grandpa. "Where do you live?"

He was starting to slouch, so he propped his hand on the open screen door to stable himself, "You ain't my daddy and it's none of your business."

I nodded, "Fair enough."

He lost his balance and began to fall; I shouted, "Woah," and caught him.

As I did, he gripped the collar of my robe and buried his face in my chest. Time froze for a moment and as we stood upright again, his body began to tremble then he began to sob. "I'm such an idiot."

I gently patted his back, "Look sport, you're not an idiot. Maybe a little overzealous, but definitely not an idiot."

Something about what I said made him grip my robe and sob harder. "No one even cares I exist, and this world would just be better off without me."

I wrapped my arms tighter around him, placed my hand behind his neck, and spoke softly. "Come on kiddo, you're way too young to be saying things like that."

"It's true." He whined.

I held him in silence for a moment. This kid I didn't even know was baring his soul to me and I had no idea what to do. Finally, we separated, and he slipped down to the porch. I caught him again; this time I shifted my arm and picked him up. With one arm around my neck and one dangling lazily beside him I carried him inside and laid him on the couch. As I pulled away, he held to the collar of my robe, our faces were only inches apart. He whispered and I could feel his breath hit my lips. "Hold me, daddy, I'm so cold."

The smell of liquor on his breath didn't even bother me. It had been years since anyone had called me "daddy" and I couldn't deny the fact that I had missed it so much... so *very* much. A flood of feelings and memories came rushing back to me. I missed being the one my little boy ran to when he was hurt. I missed my wife and the way she used to grip the collar of my shirt the way Van was doing right now. His lips parted and his eyes were closed as he lifted himself slightly. I wasn't sure what he was going to do then I could feel his soft nose nuzzle my pecs as he moaned, "You're so warm."

I tried to pull him away, "Alright sport I think you should lie back down and sleep this off."

He whined, "But you're so warm and you smell so good."

I could feel my temperature rising. It had been a

long time since I'd had any intimate contact with someone. This was wrong. He was drunk and only a couple of years older than my own son. There was no way I was about to let things escalate past the dangerous point we'd already reached.

Taking his hands into mine, I gently loosened their grip from my collar, and he drifted backward on the couch. I waited and after a moment I saw his chest begin to rise and fall; his breathing was shallow, and I knew he had succumbed to sleep at last. With his hands still in mine, I lowered them onto his stomach and grabbed a throw from a nearby chair.

As I laid it over him, my fatherly instincts kicked in and without thinking I tucked him in, untied his shoes, and pulled them off, setting them on the floor. I stepped back outside to pick up his belt which he had dropped, then I went back inside, closed the door, and locked it behind me.

I still felt the need to make sure he was going to be okay, so I watched him for a while from a chair to make sure he didn't throw up or anything. This was the easy part, but I knew he was going to be sick as a dog in the morning. I didn't know this kid at all, yet I still wished somehow, I could take away his pain but this was something he was just going to have to endure, and hopefully, he would learn a lesson from this. Maybe if I was lucky, he would be as open with me in the morning as he was tonight. Something was obviously tearing this kid up inside and my inquisitive nature desperately wanted to know what it was.

As I stood, I stretched and crossed the room to turn off the light. I paused momentarily to tousle his shaggy brown hair, "Sleep well, kid." Then I turned off the light and went back upstairs.

CHAPTEN TEN
What's Eating Van

When I woke up in the morning, my head was pounding, the room was spinning, and I felt like I was about to throw up at any second. As I was holding my head in my hands trying to figure out where I was and how I got here, a friendly voice mumbled, "Morning."

I turned to see a tall man in a robe with dark brown hair, a well-groomed beard, and mustache and was gazing at me over a cup of coffee. I groaned and rubbed my face with my hands as I said, "Where am I?"

The man took a seat in a nearby chair and set his mug down on the fancy stone coffee table, "Well kiddo, you got really drunk last night and pounded on my door as you shouted for my son JP to come outside so you could fight him."

I exhaled, "Oh crap!"

The man smirked, "What? You don't remember?"

I tried to think for a moment but the last thing I could remember was getting on the bus. The how and why I was here could not be explained so I shook my head no. The man stood and extended his hand, "Didn't think you would. By the way, I'm Roger."

I met his hand with mine, "Van."

He nodded, "I already know that part. You told me last night, amongst other things."

As he turned to walk away I stood and asked, "What other things?"

But before I could say anything else, I heaved and covered my mouth with my hands. He lifted a hand and pointed the direction he was walking, "The bathroom's this way."

I hurried after him and he opened the door. I rushed inside; my knees hit the floor and between dry heaves and ralphing my guts up, I felt like my soul was going to leave my body. A few moments later a soft knock came at the door, "You okay, bud?"

I was still trying to catch my breath as I heaved, "Yeah."

He replied, "Alright, just yell if you need help."

How did I end up here? How did I become so repressed? I can't believe I'm hugging some stranger's toilet because I was jealous of someone else's boyfriend. What the hell was I thinking? Even if Jeffrey would have been here, he would have probably called the cops anyway. I struggled to my feet, splashed some water on my face, and stared at myself in the mirror for a minute before turning away.

I'd grown up with so many different kids in the system that were now dead or in jail for various reasons. I'd vowed long ago that I would never end up the way they did. I'd prided myself on being street smart by watching the mistakes others made and choosing to focus on sports so I could get out of here and here I am, totally hungover in a total stranger's house and still didn't accomplish the thing I had set out to do. In fact, I'd single-handedly destroyed any chances I had with Jeffrey to begin with. I'd lost because of my own stupid actions and that's the hardest truth to swallow. What can I say? I'm a football player;

there is one thing I don't handle well and that's losing.

I turned the knob and stepped into the hallway. I couldn't help but notice how much nicer this house was than mine. It had high ceilings with ornate woodwork, neutral painted walls with tasteful art adorning it. I got lost staring at a picture in the hall of a big open meadow. I could hear footsteps approach behind me and turned my gaze to him. I felt bad that I had already forgotten his name and mumbled, "Thanks for letting me crash on your sofa dude."

He flashed me a half-smile, "Think nothing of it."

Silence lingered momentarily and I broke it by saying, "Cool picture."

He approached and took a sip of coffee, "It is, isn't it; one of my better ones."

I blinked and pointed, "You took this?"

He nodded, "Yep."

We stared at it in silence for a bit longer before I folded my arms across my stomach and groaned. He lifted his brow, "Still sick from the booze?"

I nodded with a pained expression and he stepped back into the bathroom for a moment. He emerged with a box of Alka Seltzer and said, "This should help."

I followed him to the kitchen. It was a big beautiful room with lots of windows to let in the sunshine. He opened one of the cabinets and pulled out a glass, then he grabbed a bottle of Evian water from the fridge, poured it into the glass, and dropped the two tabs inside. He turned to me, "Have a seat kiddo."

"*Kiddo.*" It was a fist blow to my heart. I had always dreamed of someone calling me that. He set the glass in front of me, "Drink that, it should take care of the nausea."

He turned back to the cabinet, "You probably

should eat something."

He fixed a bowl of oatmeal as I stared around the room in awkward silence, then he slid it across the table to me before taking a seat across from me with the newspaper. I swirled my spoon around it for a minute before taking a bite. I chewed it mechanically as I glanced around before swallowing. "This is pretty good," I said.

He lowered the paper and grinned, "Have you never had oatmeal before?"

I shook my head. "I'm glad you appreciate it. JP hates the stuff."

I took another bite and replied, "I like it a lot. Only shit I ever get is the cheap cereal my foster mom buys from the Dollar General."

He chuckled, "It should be good for what it costs. That's bodybuilding oatmeal with extra fiber and nuts and stuff."

"You're a bodybuilder?" I gushed.

He grinned, "I wouldn't say that, but I do take great care of my body."

I was suddenly feeling a little more talkative, "I play football for Clark High."

He smiled big, "What's your position?"

"Kicker," I said.

He lifted a hand to high five me, "Alright bud, that's a pretty important position."

I smiled.

Once I had finished my oatmeal, Roger folded the paper and sighed, "So, your folks are probably worried about you."

I waved in dismissal, "They probably haven't even noticed I'm gone."

Roger raised a brow as he stood, "Still, we should

probably get you home."

I sighed and stood. On the way to the living room, I mumbled, "I'm sorry about all of this."

Roger handed me my shoes, belt, and backpack, "It's no big deal. I'm just glad you didn't get yourself into trouble."

While I got dressed, he asked, "So, I'm just curious... why did you want to fight my son over Jeffrey?"

I laid back on the sofa, "I don't know... I guess I just thought if I showed up and got to tell Jeffrey how I felt about him he might give me another chance."

Roger replied, "I hate to break the bad news sport, but he's moved on."

I covered my face with my hands. It wasn't what I wanted to hear but it was what I needed to hear. As I gathered my things, Roger grabbed the keys from the entryway table and smiled empathetically, "I know it doesn't seem like it right now but I'm sure you'll find someone like Jeffrey who thinks the world of you.

He paused and licked his lips, "If it's any consolation you're a good-looking boy and anyone would be lucky to have a guy like you for their boyfriend."

I turned and met his gaze and as I made my way to the front door, "Do you really think so?"

He nodded, "Absolutely, now let me give you a ride home."

VAN

As we got in the car and made our way toward the house, silence lingered momentarily before I mumbled,

"Roger?"

"Yeah?"

I took a deep breath, "There's something I want to ask you about last night. You see, everything's a blur and I need to know something…"

"Shoot," he said as he tapped the steering wheel nervously.

"Did something happen between us last night?"

He swallowed hard, "Well…almost."

I covered my face with my hands and groaned, "I'm so sorry."

He placed his hand on my knee, "It's okay, sport. Things like that can happen sometimes when you're not in the right state of mind."

"I was *pretty* sloshed," I mumbled.

Silence lingered again as he turned onto my street, "If it makes you feel any better, I wouldn't have minded if it did."

I turned to him, "Really?"

He shifted in his seat and a faint smile formed on his lips, "It's been a while since I've been with anyone and you had me pretty horned up there for a moment."

I turned my gaze out the window and my heart sank a little, "I was halfway hoping something did happen."

"Hey!"

I turned my gaze to him as he continued, "I don't make a habit of taking advantage of people, especially drunk dudes who show up at my door in the middle of the night."

"Thanks for that," I said as we approached the house.

He pulled up to the curb, I stepped out and closed the door behind me. On the way to the front door, he rolled down the window and shouted, "Hey Van!"

I turned to him, "Yeah?"

He pulled a business card from his glove box and held it out to me, "Listen, if you ever need someone to talk to I'm always here to lend an ear."

I ran my fingers across his name, *Roger Richards,* and mumbled, "Thanks."

He rolled up the window and drove away but I stood there for a moment after he pulled away lost in my thoughts. He was the nicest man I'd ever met. Suddenly, images of his naked chest flooded my memory and the smell of his cologne filled my nostrils. I shook my head to snap myself out of the spell he was casting on me and started walking towards the door. As I turned the knob to go inside, I hoped he was serious about his offer because something was telling me it wasn't the last I would see of him.

ROGER

After Dropping Van off, I made my way back home. I couldn't help but think it was nice having someone to talk to with common interests. I love my son, JP and I'd take a bullet for him but, he's so different than me. Van is sporty and reserved with a stunning build. After our encounter last night, I definitely had to silence the devil on my shoulder goading me to fantasize about him.

I've been curious about guys for some time, but I didn't really know what I wanted until last night. I wanted someone to take care of, someone to snuggle up to at night and protect. It suddenly dawned on me that I was a true daddy, both literally and erotically. I wanted a boy. I *needed* a boy.

Even with Reggie, I felt more like a father figure to

her; always getting her out of trouble, holding her when she fell into her depressions and making sure she had everything she needed to be happy. Our romantic life had always been pretty vanilla and it was great but, I think once you've been together a long time the passion slowly dies and your relationship evolves with maturity. At least it did with us. Sometimes I regret not trying new things when she wanted me to but, making love with a woman, for me, I imagine is different than having sex with a man.

I'd read somewhere that while daddy kink can sometimes be about a balance of power, rewards for co-operation, and discipline for insubordination, it can also lean more towards recreating the traditional father/son dynamic. I suppose sex is ultimately subjective, I don't want to be just a Dom to some submissive boy, I want to be a teacher, a friend, a guide to a lost soul who's just trying to figure out who he is as a man.

The thought of some hot young buck deliberately doing something to piss me off just so I'll spank him is pretty damn hot but, I need something far beyond the physical. I need an emotional connection first and when the time is right for things to move to the next level, I'll be there to show him a world of pleasure and ecstasy far beyond his physical body and mind can handle.

When I got home, I made myself comfortable on the sofa with my laptop. It was time to learn more about this new realization. I went to my dating website and changed my criteria; "*boys seeking daddies*". I spent the next hour drooling over the images before me. Somewhere along the way, I'd ventured off to some NSFW blogs and I was too turned on to keep going so I decided to excuse myself to my room to fantasize about what I'd been missing out on all of these years.

The day had slowly slipped into the evening. Van had slept to almost one in the afternoon and once I'd tamed my lustful desires, I ended up falling asleep. I normally don't take naps during the day, but I was exhausted having stayed up watching Van most of the night making sure he was going to be okay. After I called JP, I went to the gym to workout, stopped to grab some healthy take-out then made my way back home. With JP over at Jeffrey's again, it would be another quiet evening all alone watching TV. I wasn't really watching it though; it was more for comfort, another sound in the house to distract me from my thoughts.

It wasn't working. I kept replaying the talk JP and I had over and over in my mind. I needed to talk to Reggie and the only way was to take his suggestion and write her that letter. I'd been keeping a piece of paper on my desk for just that purpose. In case the words came, I would be prepared but so far I hadn't written a single word.

I picked up the blank piece of paper and it was like something came over me... I could feel her presence around me. Commercials came on the TV for things she used to like. First, it was the one with her favorite shampoo, I could practically smell her coconut scented hair. Then, the one advertising the new Karaoke Superstars game, the one with the mom who looks just like Reggie. I suddenly couldn't take the memories any longer. I stood and made my way to the kitchen to splash some water on my face.

I ended up getting distracted by the sight outside my kitchen window. The sun was setting and as it slowly darkened the sky, light snow began to fall. Reggie used to love to watch the snow fall from the kitchen window. I took a deep breath as I made my way to the table, picked up the blank piece of paper, and ventured upstairs to my office. I took a seat and like a dam cracking under the pressure of the floodwaters behind it, my soul opened up and the words I needed to say came rushing out of me.

My Dearest Reg,

A lot has happened over the past couple of months. JP and I sold the house and we moved across the river to Indiana. I know I should have told you sooner, but I just couldn't take the pain of the memories of the life we built together anymore. The new house is very nice. You probably wouldn't like it; it's one of those old houses that have been modernized and I know you're a stickler for authenticity.

JP likes it though, and it's easier on me to keep clean since it's much smaller and efficient. It sits across the street from a quaint little bakery, which I know you would have really loved. The owner is a single lady named Dana, who has also lost her spouse. She has a son around JP's age and they have really hit it off. I smile because I remember how much you wanted a gay son. They make a cute couple; Jeffrey is a good boy, a little clumsy maybe, but in an adorable way.

JP and I had a really bad argument recently that brought a lot of underlying issues to the surface. I wish you were here to make it all better as you always were the glue that held our "group of weirdos" together. He said I should write you a letter, that maybe it will help me heal but until now I didn't know what to say.

I tried to pretend for the longest time that everything was okay, but I was just living a lie, going through the motions of life, and ignoring any stress. But I can't deny the truth any longer; I am so... alone. This isn't what I bargained for and I know it sounds selfish, but I shouldn't be raising a kid by my-

self. Sometimes I get so scared about not being able to do a good job raising him and other times I get angry wondering why this happened to me.

As if all of that wasn't enough, lately I've been having these feelings I can no longer ignore. I thought this would be easier to say but... it isn't. Reggie... I'm attracted to guys. Romantically.

If you were still alive, I would probably just shove these desires back deep inside where they've always been, but, with you gone, these feelings are all I have left. They're literally <u>all</u> I have now, and I don't know what to do with them. Part of me wants to explore them further but, the other half of my heart makes me feel like a criminal, makes me feels like... like I'm a shitty person for cheating on you.

I know you're not here to tell me it's okay for me to move on, but, if you were still here then I wouldn't be writing you this letter. I guess what I am trying to say is I can't take the loneliness anymore. JP is growing up fast and I imagine he and Jeffrey will graduate, move out, pursue their relationship... maybe even get married at some point?

Where do I fit into that picture Reggie?

There are so many years left and I don't know how or what is the right way to fill them...

The flood of tears became so overwhelming by this point that I could no longer see what I was writing, the large droplets staining the page, mixing with the ink. I dropped my pen and cradled my head in my hands.

I was so strong for *so* long... I didn't even cry at the funeral. I swallowed my emotions, thinking I needed to be brave and strong for my boy so as not to upset him. I still remember that day like it was yesterday. After it was all over and it was just me and him standing there beside

Reggie's casket, he turned to me, "Aren't you going to cry, dad?"

I just shook my head and mumbled, "Not right now, son. I'm sure it will hit me later." But later never came… until now. The emptiness of the house echoed with my sobs. Oh God, what am I going to do?

A sudden wave of calm came over me as I lowered my hands onto the desk and stared at the gold band around my finger for the longest time. I played with it for a minute before finally, slowly, sliding it off. I placed it in the center of the letter, carefully folded it up and placed the little package inside one of the tiny cubby drawers in my antique desk, and slowly closed it.

CHAPTER ELEVEN
Something About a Boy

OMG, where have you been? So, a lot has been happening, as you know JP and I have been having sleepovers for a while now. They have all been innocent up to this point; like two best friends who listen to music and talk about all of our hopes and dreams despite my many attempts to entice him, but something is different about tonight.

It's the weekend before Christmas, JP has been very quiet today, like something is on his mind, but every time we tried to talk about it, mom interrupted. She had a series of festive holiday events planned which all started with us fishing out the holiday decorations from the attic. You should have seen JP's face when he saw mom's pink Christmas tree and pastry themed ornaments. I didn't even try to pretend it was normal and he admitted it was actually really pretty when she finished decorating it.

After the tree was finished, we prepped sugar cookies then we ate lunch while they baked. As the cookies cooled on racks, we were finally able to get a moment to chat but he was very elusive. "Is everything okay?" I asked.

"Sure." He shrugged.

His unwillingness to communicate was frustrating. I tried my best to sound nice, but the harder I tried, the worse I made things. "You're acting strange today. We're

BFF's. You can tell me anything!"

He snarled, "I don't want to talk it about it, okay?"

We decorated the cookies in awkward silence while mom ran to the store to grab a few things for dinner. When she got back, she could see JP and I weren't talking. Never one to leave things alone, she let a few moments pass as she put things away then turned to us, "Alright, I'm not going to leave you boys alone anymore if you two aren't going to play nice. What's going on?"

I don't know why I felt the need to protect JP even though I was technically mad at him. I forced a smile, "What do you mean? We're just super focused on decorating the cookies, see?"

I held one up for her inspection and she arched a brow before turning to JP, "Oh, would you look at that… whatever it is."

JP squinted and mumbled, "It's a zombie gingerbread man."

Mom chuckled nervously, "Of *course* it is, and I see he is even eating a little gumdrop brain from the gingerbread man next to him!"

JP lifted his eyes and mumbled, "That's not his mouth, that's his eye."

Mom looked disturbed but still managed to force admiration that only a mother could pull off, "Isn't that a little low for an eye?"

"It slid down." He mumbled.

Mom patted his shoulder as he walked away, "Alrighty then."

"Do you mind if I step outside to get some fresh air?"

Mom replied from across the room, "Not at all JP. You go right ahead."

He threw his hood over his head, slumped his shoulders, then tucked his hands into the pockets of his hoodie. As he passed by, I asked, "Do you mind if I go with you?"

He sneered, "It's a free country."

"So is Canada." I quipped. What's your point?"

"*Whatever*," he retorted as he shuffled toward the front of the house.

I stood to go after him and mom spun around, "Hold it right there. What's going on between you and JP? A few weeks ago, you were practically planning the wedding?"

I whimpered, "I have no idea. He woke up like this and he's been all dark and depressed ever since."

She thought for a minute and held up a finger as the "a-ha" moment occurred, "The best way to find out why a boy is acting a certain way is to find out if his father gets the same way."

I gushed, "Great idea mom."

She pulled her phone from her pocket, then pushed its center button. "Siri, call Roger," she said as she put it on speakerphone. It rang a few times before he answered, "Hi Dana, what's up? Is everything okay with the boys?"

She hesitated, "Well, they've had some kind of spat, and I'm not sure what it's over. Jeffrey says JP woke up all dark and depressed this morning and has been very moody ever since."

Roger sighed, "Oh boy. Well, he gets like this sometimes. I better come get him before phase two of this downward spiral commences."

I whimpered, "It gets worse?"

Roger heard me and chuckled, "Much worse. Has he started answering questions with single words like *sure*, *okay*, or *whatever*?"

Mom glanced at me and I nodded; she replied, "Yep."

"On my way," Roger replied quickly then hung up.

Mom met my gaze, "Sweetie, you better go sit with him until Roger gets here."

"But I don't want him to go home." I cried.

Mom frowned, "I know baby, but we don't know him well enough yet to know how to deal with something like this."

I sighed and made my way to the front door and glanced out to see where JP was. He was sitting on the porch step with a stick drawing circles in the snow. I opened the door and made my way to where he was sitting. "Do you mind if I sit down?"

"No."

We sat in silence for a minute before he mumbled, "In case you're wondering, you didn't do anything wrong."

I turned to him and he met my gaze. Then he grabbed my hand and held onto it tightly before turning his focus back to the snow he was drawing in and we sat in silence until his dad pulled into the driveway. When he saw his dad's car he turned to me, "What's dad doing here? I thought he wasn't supposed to come until tomorrow."

I turned my gaze to the ground, "Mom and I thought you might be happier at home, that is, until you feel better."

I lifted my eyes and he flashed me a half-smile as I continued, "I hope it was okay."

He leaned in and kissed my cheek, but he lingered for a few seconds before he pulled my way. I closed my eyes to bask in his kiss and as he pulled away, I opened them. "Thank you," he whispered.

Part of me wished he would change his mind and decide to stay but I understood something was wrong and like mom said, this was something he really needed to work through with his dad.

As Roger got out of the car, JP stood and ran towards him. I watched from the porch as he stood in front of his dad looking like a sad little sack of potatoes, then hugged him. His dad's eyes widened and he stared straight ahead as he gently rested his arms around his son's shoulders. "Just let me get my stuff and I'll be right out!" he called as they separated and he breezed past me and back into the house. I continued sitting on the steps, propped my hands under my chin, and sighed. His dad sauntered over to where I was sitting and sat down beside me with a grunt, "Hi Jeffrey."

I mumbled, "Hi."

He cleared his throat, "I'm sorry JP isn't feeling well. He gets like this sometimes and just needs a day or two to escape and work out whatever problem is on his mind."

I turned to him and mumbled, "Do you think he'll be okay to come back for Christmas Eve dinner with you?"

Roger shrugged. "We'll have to see. I hope once I talk to him he'll open up and tell me what's wrong."

I sighed. "I understand."

He placed his hand on my knee, "You're a good guy Jeffrey. It takes a special kind of person to step back and give the person they care about space. I used to have to do the same thing when…when um… JP's mom got like this."

I stared at him with an inquisitive expression, "JP's mom used to get like this too?"

Roger nodded, "Yep. She suffered from manic depression and would often get like this without any warning."

I lowered my head again. I could hear my mom behind us asking JP if he had everything, then he opened the screen door and stepped outside. Roger stood and turned around, "You ready to go sport?"

JP nodded silently then sprinted to their car. Roger

lingered for a moment and talked to my mom. Her tone sounded worried as she greeted him, "Roger, I'm so sorry we had to call but we weren't sure what else to do."

Roger smiled at her, "I'm glad you did. His mom used to get like this too and I was just telling Jeffrey that when this happens, it's best just to step back and let them work through it on their own."

Mom sighed, "Oh goodness, bless his little heart. I hate to see people sad at Christmas."

"He'll come around soon I'm sure. I'm hoping once he gets home and gets comfortable he'll open up and talk to me about what's troubling him."

Mom smiled, "I certainly hope so. We're getting pretty used to having him around the house. Oh, that reminds me, will you and he be able to make it for dinner on Christmas Eve?"

"I sure hope so, but I'll call you if anything changes or he's not feeling up to it."

"Good deal," she said as she turned her focus to me.

"Why don't we go inside and finish decorating those cookies, Jeffrey?"

ROGER

On the way home I decided to take a chance and open up about how my weekend went in hopes JP would return the favor. I cleared my throat, "Well, aren't we quite the pair. I'm feeling a little melancholy myself. I had a very interesting weekend."

JP turned to me and cocked his head to the side, "Really, what happened?"

I grinned, "Yeah, last night a boy came by the house looking for you and Jeffrey."

JP shifted, "Who was it?"

I glanced at him, "A kid named Van?"

"Van Wishnevski from the football team! What the hell did he want?" he shouted.

I scowled at him, "Language!"

"Sorry," he mumbled.

Silence lingered between us for a minute before I continued, "It seems he wanted to challenge you to a fight for Jeffrey's love."

JP sat straight up, "WHAT? Van Wishnevski likes dudes…and he likes Jeffrey? Jeffrey's my boyfriend! Take me to his house!"

I grinned, "You're really fired up about someone you were upset with a few minutes ago."

JP froze like a deer in headlights and turned to look out the window as he mumbled, "This has nothing to do with Jeffrey."

"You want to tell me what it has to do with?"

He sighed, "I'm just so scared okay?"

He glanced at me then back at the window, "Dad?"

"Yeah?" I replied.

"How did you feel before your first time with mom?"

I cleared my throat and shifted, "Well son, those are two different questions."

He turned back to me and his eyes widened, "You mean your first time *wasn't* with mom?"

I shook my head no. "I was hoping this conversation could wait a couple more years but I think you're ready."

I saw him out of the corner of my eye. He was hanging on my every word. It was the first time in a long time I felt like we had or were about to make a connection the way dads should with their sons. I continued, "My first time was with a guy."

JP's mouth hung open from shock, "You never told me that!"

I shrugged, "It never came up."

"Who was it? What happened?" He was firing out questions like bullets from a gun.

I began, "I was about your age, and my friend Chad and I had been hanging out for a long time. We used to go camping, fishing, all kinds of stuff like that. We were driving down this country highway that led out the lake. No Doubt was playing on the radio and I could sense something was different between us."

JP interrupted, "That's how I've been feeling with Jeffrey lately."

I needed to figure out a way to prolong our conversation so I turned down a side street with a sign labeled Indiana Scenic Byway. Slowly, the houses and businesses began to disappear and I could see the river bend in the distance. I could hear Reggie's voice in my mind, *"Ooh, down there; let's go on an adventure!"*

She used to love cruising and just getting lost out in the country somewhere. I smiled and thanked her in my mind; it was as if she was my navigator steering me the perfect way down the curvy highway that led to our son's heart.

He was so lost right now and the only way to find him was to use the maps that had been inside of me all along and those maps were the memories of my own troubled adolescence and all the emotions I felt before I took those first steps into the unknown waters of manhood.

You never forget the first time you *feel*. The first time you realize there is more behind the confusion and insecurity that comes with being a teenage boy. Deep inside of your heart are desires that are burning to become more than just taboo fantasies. We are all just humans longing to know we are loved; that we're not weird. Chad was that person for me.

JP interrupted my thoughts as he sighed, "Wow!"

I turned to glance out the window. The sun was setting over the river's bend. "Can we stop dad?"

He turned to me with hopeful eyes and I pulled over to the side of the highway onto the shoulder. We opened the doors and walked to the edge of the road where the guardrail protected cars from slipping into the current. The December air coming from the water was tinged with ice. Our breath expelled into the air as we admired the picturesque scene.

After a few minutes, JP asked, "So your first time was with a boy?"

"Yep," I said as I stared out across the water.

"How did it happen, dad?"

I took a deep breath and closed my eyes as I remembered. I felt chills run down my spine as I whispered, "It was the end of summer. Chad and I were coming home from a weekend camping trip."

I opened my eyes and hesitated, "We pulled over on the side of the highway... because we could see a river down below the tree line."

I could feel JP's eyes locked on me, "We jumped out of the car and he ran ahead of me, stripping off his clothes as he did. I don't know what came over me but I just followed his lead. Before long we were both naked.
We stopped at the end of a little wooden dock and he took my hand."

I was suddenly feeling emotional. JP whispered, "What happened next?"

I squinted and mumbled, "We jumped, and when we came back up we were face to face."

I turned to JP," Then our lips met in a kiss; one of those sloppy fast kisses where you're just desperately searching for one another's mouth. He tasted so good, his breath was so hot and his skin was so wet and I remember thinking I never wanted it to end.

After a few moments, I climbed back up on the dock. I was sitting with my legs dangling; he was still in the water between them and I stretched down my arms to lift him out. He used my body to push himself out and on top of me."

I closed my eyes again. My breath was shallow as I continued, "I remember everything about him. His skin was so soft and smooth. I remember the way my hands glided down his body, the wayward beads of water dripping from his shaggy blonde hair and tracing lines down his cheek. We kissed again and our tongues danced before he separated and drifted lower, showering my body in kisses as he descended."

JP sighed, "Woah, *dad*!"

I turned to him with a nervous smile, "It was beautiful and I'll never forget him. Just like you'll never forget the first time you and Jeffrey do something."

JP diverted his eyes, "Whatever happened to Chad?"

My voice cracked as I replied, "He moved away and I never saw him again. Sometimes I wonder if he still remembers me. If he still thinks about me the way I do him."

JP covered his face and his body began to shake as he started to cry. I wrapped my arms around him, "Aw, JP, buddy, what's wrong?"

He gasped a few times and pulled away, wiping his eyes as he did, "That's what I'm afraid of."

"What?" I mumbled.

He shouted, "That I'll give myself to him, and then I'll never see him again."

I hugged him again, "Oh JP you don't have to worry about that. Jeffrey's mom has a thriving business and they've lived here for many years."

JP heaved, "I know but I just can't shake all these fears: What if I'm no good? What if we do something and it changes things?"

I rubbed his back, "Oh JP you can't let worry destroy the best moments of your life. When the time comes for you and Jeffrey to take things to the next level trust me you'll know, and there will be nothing you can do to stop it. That's how love works; you never know when it's going to strike but when it does, it's one of the most wonderful things a boy can experience."

We separated and he wiped away his tears, "I like him a lot and all weekend I knew he wanted to do something but I just wasn't ready."

I stooped to one knee and met his gaze, "And you know what?"

"What?" he said.

"It's okay if you're not ready. You don't have to be in a rush to fall in love or to feel like you have to do something with Jeffrey. Everyone matures in their own time and if you aren't ready yet, you need to talk to him, but never compromise your principles just because you feel like you have to do something."

I smiled at him, and he smiled at me, "Thanks, dad."

"You're welcome, sport."

I stood, "Now, that we got all of that sorted out, what do you say we go home."

JP chirped, "Sounds like a plan to me."

Once we were in the car his stomach growled and he turned to me, "Maybe we can stop and get something to eat?"

My stomach growled in reply to his and we shared a laugh. We paused momentarily, stared at one another then erupted in a fit of laughs again. Once we had regained our composure I started the car, "Sounds like a plan to me."

On the way back to the city the day had turned into night as I finished telling JP about my encounter with Van. I turned on the radio and I shouted at the sound of a familiar tune, "Katy Perry, Teenage Dream!"

I started singing and JP joined in. My little boy wasn't my little boy anymore... he was my little *man*.

EPILOGUE

Dear Diary,

    Christmas Eve came and I was starting to worry JP and his dad weren't coming. My heart was officially broken. I hadn't heard from him since our little incident the day before and I still couldn't figure out what happened but, all I knew was without JP, my life wouldn't feel so happy.

    Over the past month, he had become my reason for living, my BFF, my *everything*. Mom tried to convince me that I didn't do anything wrong, but I still wasn't sure. She had talked to his dad Roger a few times but he couldn't give a definite answer as to whether or not they would be able to make it.

    Mom and I were sitting on the couch watching Home Alone when she turned to me, "I hate seeing you so sad at Christmas."

    "I'm sorry," I mumbled.

    She made her way to the Christmas tree and grabbed a present, "Why don't you open one of your presents; it might make you feel better."

    I crossed my arms. "The only present I want is JP".

    Mom frowned and set the present back under the tree before crossing the room to go to the front door. She glanced outside, "Would you look at that. It's starting to snow."

    She closed the door, then stopped by the thermostat to turn up the heat before sitting back down and covering back up with a throw. I was lost in my thoughts as the TV droned in the background. A knock came at the door prompting me to jump. Mom mumbled from inside of a book, "Could you see who that is sweetie?"

I stood and crossed the room. As I opened the door I saw a face peer up from inside of a hoodie. He was holding a present and as he looked up, he met my gaze with a coy smile that shattered my heart like glass. I flung open the door, burst into tears, and wrapped my arms tightly around his neck as I said, "I thought you weren't coming."

We separated and I rested my forehead against his, "I thought you were mad at me."

He whispered, "I could never be mad at you, you're my boyfriend and I love you."

Fangirl scream! I just melted like a snowman on the beach. My eyes widened and I mumbled, "What did you just say?"

He smirked, "That you're my boyfriend and I love you." He held out the gift, "I got you something?"

Mom shouted from inside, "Who is it, sweetie?"

I shouted, "It's JP mom!"

Mom shouted in reply, "OMG, hurry up and get in here! You're letting all the cold in."

I met JP's gaze and took the gift, "Thank you!"

He blushed and diverted his gaze, "I um, I wanted to give you something else too."

He leaned in; his eyes were half-closed. I knew what was coming but this time he wasn't going for my cheek. He was coming straight at me. I hugged the gift and closed my eyes. Time stood still and I felt them; his sweet lips pressed tightly to mine and my soul briefly left my body.

Slowly he pulled away and I took the opportunity

to nip at that delicious lip ring he always wore. "Ow," he said and covered it with his hand.

"I'm so sorry; it was just something I'd always dreamed of doing."

"It's okay." He giggled.

As we went inside I asked, "Where's your dad?"

"He always stops by the cemetery to visit mom on Christmas Eve."

"I'm sorry," I said with a somber tone.

JP smiled, "It's okay."

Silence lingered for a moment before he shouted excitedly, "Aren't you going to open your present?"

I rushed to the couch and plopped down and he sat next to me. I tore away the wrapping paper and slid the lid off the box; it was a black hoodie.

Mom was in the kitchen grabbing some appetizers as he explained, "I know you've wanted to take our relationship to the next level and… I want to as well but, I'm just not ready yet. I want to take things slow and when the moment is right then we'll know."

I was a little disheartened but still, I smiled then pulled the hoodie from the box. He grinned, "Smell it."

I arched my brow and leaned in; it smelled like him. I hugged it to my body and searched his expression for an explanation. He took my chin between his thumb and finger, "I understand us being young and having urges, but until we are ready I wanted to help you so I took my favorite hoodie and sprayed it with my cologne so every time you need to "take care of things" you can wear this and it's like I'm there with you."

My lip trembled and I whimpered, "Aw… JP!"

He leaned in again and met my lips in another kiss. This time it was long and sensual; his hand rested gently on my cheek as he touched the tip of my tongue with his. Mom emerged from around the counter and covered her eyes, "Woah! Sorry to interrupt!"

JP bit his bottom lip and glanced around nervously as I scowled at mom. She grinned as she set a cheese platter on the table along with some mini cherry Danish before turning to make her way back to the kitchen. I fell back on the sofa, JP followed and we stared at the tree for a minute before I felt him take my hand.

ROGER

I pulled into the cemetery and followed the drive to where Reggie's body rested. I couldn't bear to come here except for a few times a year; her birthday, Mother's Day, Christmas. I parked and stood before the headstone etched with her name, *Regina Rose Richards, beloved wife, and mother.*

The wind picked up and blew my scarf around my neck. I couldn't help but think it was her way of saying hello from beyond the grave. When she was alive she always adjusted my tie or scarf depending on the season or occasion.

I had brought the letter I had written with me along with a letter from JP to tuck inside of her flower vase along with a big bouquet of poinsettias. Normally, I wouldn't be so nosy but ever since he told me about his journal I was curious about the things he was saying to her. I tucked my letter in the vase, then positioned the flowers before pulling his from my pocket.

As I began to read I felt tears welling up in my eyes...

Dear Journal/Mom,
Merry Christmas from the living world; I just wanted to

let you know this will be my last letter. You see, I've fallen in love with a boy named Jeffrey and he makes me feel alive. Before I met him, I didn't feel like there was anyone I could talk to about all the things I was feeling so I wrote to you.

But now I have him so you don't have to worry about me anymore. Also, things have changed between dad and me; last night he opened up and we talked about some important things going on in my life. He shared things about his life that helped me make the most important decision a boy can make and that was whether to have my first time. I decided I wasn't ready.

You see, I'm still a boy and I'm not ready to grow up just yet and if I have sex with Jeffrey I know everything will change. Dad still needs me to get through some problems he's about to face and I want to be there to return the favor if and when he needs me to help. He's a good man and I'm not sure how you got him in bed to make me because he is sooo gay, but I couldn't be more thankful that you were my mom and he is my dad.

I love you always and forever.
Your little wallflower, JP.

I folded the letter, tucked it into Reggie's vase, kissed my hand, and ran it over the lettering of her name, "Merry Christmas darling."

JEFFREY

Later in the evening when JP's dad showed up, we ate dinner, opened presents, and watched a Christmas movie before saying goodnight. I really wanted JP to spend the night but mom didn't think it was a good idea since the bakery reopens the day after tomorrow and JP's dad has to go back to work. She thought it was best if JP and I have a day off to spend with our parents. Mom did say that JP was welcome to meet us at the bakery in the next morning, so at least we have that.

I always hate this part. I've never been good at saying goodbye. It's one of the saddest things we as human beings have to do. I've learned a lot about myself this year and you've learned a lot about what makes a clumsy sixteen-year-old gay boy tick. JP's dad is taking us down to the riverfront to see the fireworks on New Year's Eve and I have to say that I am so excited for the coming year. There's a lot of hope and love out there and I'm okay waiting for the moment when JP decides to take things to the next level. In the meantime, I'm just going to be me.

It's like mom always says, we don't have to be in a rush to fall in love, just enjoy every moment, every touch, and every laugh and if you find yourself feeling alone like you'll never find someone to call your own just grab yourself a cherry Danish and know that you always have a friend inside the pages of this diary of a baker's son.

THE END
(for now)

ABOUT THE AUTHOR

Daniel Elijah Sanderfer

Daniel Elijah Sanderfer is a retired Hospitality Manager who currently resides in Southern Indiana with his husband William. Originally from the Blue Ridge Mountain region of Virginia, he moved to Indiana to be closer to his then-fiance. They have been married for three years and together for sixteen total years. He was always interested in writing even from a young age and was featured in a few poetry collections as a teen. Now he has over thirty published works available on Amazon.

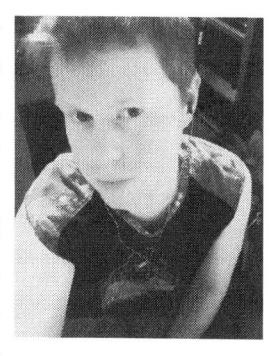

When he is not writing he is a caretaker, as his husband is disabled and requires full-time care. He also enjoys going to antique stores, and in the summer he enjoys going to yard sales and being outdoors in his garden. He currently writes LGBT fiction that covers many different tropes and genres. The best place to keep up with Daniel is on social media, specifically in his Facebook group Sanderfer's Socialites.

Printed in Great Britain
by Amazon